Dangerous Commitments

By:

Isis

www.calliepublishing.com

Dangerous Indulgences Copyright © 2020 by Isis

Dedicated to my Mommie, Angela Kelly. May she rest peacefully in heaven. #TKcA

Dedicated to J3 and my tribe. Thanks for holding me down and being the inspiration that I need during tough times, for the jokes that keep me laughing, and for the prayers that keep me centered.

To my readers, thanks for being so loyal. There are more great stories to come! You are appreciated. Love you always!

Prelude

I was annoyed by the sounds of raindrops hitting my window. It was bizarre because I usually like the sound of rain, but with this migraine every noise irritated me. It was also making me nauseous. Or was it something else? Today was such a crazy day. Two tests were positive, and then one came back negative. I don't even know if I'm pregnant, and my doctor can't see me for another three weeks. How can I go for three weeks without knowing if there is a baby in my womb? He doesn't even know, and I'm not sure I want to tell him. I've been pregnant before and lost the baby in college. The symptoms I feel now are very similar. All I want to do is sleep, but I can't quiet these thoughts in my head.

I pulled the throw from the back of the couch and wrapped it around myself. The house was completely dark and I welcomed the silence. My roommate was gone for the night. She had taken care of me during the day, but now my thoughts ran wild in the stillness. How did I even end up here? How could I have been so reckless?

The pounding in my head began to subside. Migraines are truly a pain from the deepest pits of hell. My phone beeped. Who in the hell could be texting me at 3 AM?

Bae: You up?
Me: Unfortunately
Bae: I want you.

That's all he ever had to say. That's why I'm in this predicament right now. I responded, "Come thru."
Then there was a knock on the door. I laughed out loud. He was truly something. I was already naked. Who sleeps in clothes? As soon as I opened the door, his eyes went to my breasts.

"Hey," I said sheepishly, as if he had never seen me naked before.
"Hey," he replied, closing the door behind him.
He pulled me close and held me in a tight embrace.
"I've missed you," he whispered in my ear.
I felt so small in his arms. I rubbed my hands up and down his back and sighed. He made me feel so safe.

We hugged for what seemed like an eternity. I let him go and took his hand. I'm sure he wanted to head to the bedroom so I led him there. There were no words. I undressed him slowly and kissed every inch of him while doing so. I was about to take off his underwear when he stopped me.
"We don't have to have sex, I just want to hold you," he said. That comment took me completely off guard. We'd been having sex incessantly for the past few months.
He pulled me into the bed and held me closely. His arms engulfed my small frame. He was a giant compared to me. We laid in silence and I could feel his heartbeat on my back. I really wanted to tell him about the pregnancy, but I was afraid of what he would say. I wasn't sure how I even felt about it. I wrestled with these thoughts as I looked at the clock on the nightstand.

It was 3:24 A.M. He wasn't sleeping. His breathing didn't indicate sleep, so I decided to probe him. I turned around to face him. I rubbed his chest and had to talk myself into having this conversation.
"Hey you," I whispered.
"Yeah," he replied.
"Are you sleep?"
I know, it's the dumbest fucking question to ask someone, but I was building up to drop this bomb.
"No," he replied and began to rub my back.
My heart began to beat fast, and he pulled me closer, placing his hand on my chest.
 "I think I'm pregnant," I blurted out.
"You are," he replied.

Wait! What? I didn't even know what to say. I didn't say anything. He kissed me on my forehead and then said, "and it's a boy."

Chapter One: Fix It!!!

We were standing on the bridge overlooking the lake. The sun was beginning to set and the amber rays were hitting my face. I placed my hand on my cheek and it was warm. The blue waters were hypnotizing and I found myself getting lost in the rhythms. The scenery was beautiful, picturesque, as if it belonged on a postcard. The waves were slowly forming and their sounds became melodies to our ears, blocking out the rest of the world.

We stood in awe of creation, not wanting to spoil the moment with trivial words. I felt his arms wrap around me. I closed my eyes and inhaled his cologne. Why was he so nervous? His heart was beating way too fast. I hoped he was not backing out. We made up our minds and made plans months ago. This was a huge step for us both, and it needed to be done. I sighed, not wanting to speak, but I needed to figure out if he was getting cold feet. I didn't want to do this alone. I needed his support.

"What's wrong baby?" I asked softly.
"Are you sure we're doing the right thing?" he asked.
"We've been over this a million times. Are you getting cold feet?"
"A little."
"Listen, we agreed to be together forever right?"
"Right!"
"So taking this step is about forever,"
"Ok. I love you," he said and kissed me on top of my head.
I didn't respond. I held his hands that were around my waist and took one last look at the sunset. It was magical and there was no one I'd rather share this moment with.
"Are you ready to jump?" I asked.

"Ready whenever you are," he replied.
He stood on the ledge first, and then held my hand as I climbed next to him. This leap was symbolic, the beginning of forever. I heard the crowd countdown, "3, 2, 1 jump!"

I jumped from out of my sleep. Why in the hell was I jumping off of a bridge with Colin of all people? What did this dream mean?

Colin

I paced the room. She sat on the floor weeping. I didn't know if I should be angry or relieved. The mahogany grandfather clock in the master bedroom ticked echoing our silence. The sound was beginning to give me a headache. I sat across from her and snatched the paper from her hand. She began to cry loudly, but I ignored her. I read the first line over and over again.

Colin Mena is excluded as the biological father.

I sat in disbelief with my head in my hand.
"Why Carmen? Just why?"
I panted holding back my tears. She just kept crying. It felt as if someone hit me in the chest. How could she betray me like this? Then I began to cry.

I was looking forward to being a father. Colin Jr. was so perfect, and he brought me so much joy. I guess deep in my heart that I knew he wasn't mine, I've always had doubts, but I wanted him to be mine so badly that I ignored those doubts and gave her my all. I thought I was doing the right thing by marrying her, even told her we could elope, but she wanted a fairy tale wedding and wanted to wait until she lost the baby weight.

I would have given her the world because she had my son, and now it was all a lie. I clenched my teeth as my heart began to pound. Now I was angry. I stood up slowly and walked over to her. She cowered and although every fiber in me wanted to smack the shit out of her, I just pulled her up and hugged her. She held me tightly and cried into my chest soaking my shirt. This was unbelievable, yet I had the urge to comfort her despite it all.

"I'm so sorry Colin," she sobbed into my chest. I didn't say anything.
She wasn't a bad person, so I knew that she was being sincere. Of course, she wanted me to be the father. I was really all she had. We had a beautiful home and she didn't have a care in the world. I just held her. The pain was becoming unbearable.
"I'm leaving," I whispered.
"I know," she whimpered.

I pulled her back and looked into her eyes. The woman that stood before me looked like a stranger. I couldn't believe I had spent the last three years with her. I knew that I had to go to Chicago. Go to Iris. I had broken her heart for this, for a lie. I packed my bags in silence as her eyes followed me. Her sobs snuck out from behind her knees, as she lay curled up on the bed. The more I heard the more anger built inside of me.

Cheating is one thing, but for her to pass off a child as mine, that was low. I couldn't bear to look at her anymore. I grabbed my keys, bag, phone, and walked out of the door. I didn't know what I was going to do about the divorce, the house, the cars-I just knew I needed to go to Iris. I needed to explain to her that I was wrong and that she was the one all along. I just hoped that she would forgive me.

I pulled up to the airstrip hoping my buddy with his plane was available. I parked my car and went looking for him.

"Hey Jett," I yelled out.
"What's up C?" he walked towards me.

"I need a lift to Chicago."

He looked at my bags and then looked back into my eyes. "What happened? Thought you were about to be a family man?"

Jett had given me rides to Chicago before. He knew I had a girl there.

"Well the baby isn't mine," I solemnly replied.

He walked towards me and we embraced.

"Damn man. That's fucked up," he said in a hug.

"I know, but I have to make things right with my girl now."

"Alright. You're lucky I want some pizza. Just get me a room and we're even."

I couldn't wait to get to Iris. I was afraid of what she may say, or if she would take me back at all. I knew she was dating Sebastian, but somehow I needed to convince her that I needed her and that she needed me. We were too old to play these games. I fucked up big time, and getting her to forgive me and take me back was my mission. These thoughts haunted me, and I had to get my head together. I got on board, took a shot of whiskey, some Benadryl, and then went to sleep. Luckily his jet had a bed so I was able to sleep the entire four-hour ride. No turbulence was a plus!

I didn't know what I was going to say to Iris. We hadn't talked in months and I knew she hated me. I hated myself for hurting her. When the plane landed I took a car to her house and noticed that B's car was also outside. I needed to be alone with her. I needed to plead my case and tell her that she was whom I wanted all along. It was pouring down raining and cold in Chicago. I was not dressed for this type of weather. I ran to the door and tried to use the code she had given me months ago. It didn't work. Damn! I had to ring the bell.

She opened the door and was shocked.

"Colin, what are you doing here?" she asked.

I didn't have any words. I just held her. Held her tight. She relaxed in my arms and it felt good to just hold her.

"What are you doing here?" she asked again.

"I want you back. I need you back," I replied.

"Didn't you marry your baby mama?" I could hear the hurt in her voice.
"I need to tell you something," I replied about to pour my heart out to her, but the door opened behind me.

B and Sasha came into the house. B hugged me, but I watched Sasha show Iris a pregnancy test. They headed to the bathroom.
"Is that a pregnancy test?" I asked. I didn't know who it was for.
I couldn't even hear her response. They went into the bathroom and slammed the door. My head was spinning. Was my baby pregnant? Was I too late? No. It had to be for Sasha.

I paced outside of the door, mind racing. When the door opened I asked Sasha if she was pregnant. She looked at me like I was crazy.
"It wasn't for her, it was for me," Iris replied. I was taken aback.
"Wait, Iris, the baby is not mine." I explained the hospital situation and the hernia and how we found out he wasn't mine. She sat on the bed listening, but was silent. Then a timer went off. Iris and B went into the bathroom. I paced again waiting for them to come out.
"She's not pregnant!" B exclaimed.
"Let me see," Iris jumped up and grabbed the test from B's hands.
"It's definitely negative," she said as she looked at the box and then looking at the test several times. She sat on the floor with the test still in her hands. I sat next to her and hoped that my presence would comfort her a bit.

"Well, we're going to go," Sasha announced.
 B bent down and kissed Iris on the forehead. He then took Sasha by the hand and they walked out of the door.
There was an awkward silence between us. The sound of thunder and rain could be heard, but Iris didn't speak. I didn't know what to do and if I should talk to her.

I just wanted to hold her and comfort her. I was so ecstatic that she wasn't pregnant. I took her by the hand and led her into the bathroom. I started to run her a bath. She just stood on the wall.

I began to undress her. She didn't fight me. She let me remove her shorts and tank top. She wasn't wearing any underwear. I picked her up and placed her into the water. She leaned her head back on the tub pillow and closed her eyes. I lit the candles that were on the side of the tub and turned on some music. I then went into the kitchen to pour her a glass of wine. I handed it to her and she whispered, "Thank you," in the smallest voice I've ever heard from her.

I was baffled. Was she upset that she wasn't pregnant? Meaning that she wanted to have a baby by Sebastian. I began to feel tense and upset. I needed to talk to her to see where her head was. I had just dropped a bomb on her and now this. I'm sure she was overwhelmed.

"Colin?" she whispered.
"Yes, baby?" I asked as I knelt next to the tub.
"So you left your wife and came here to me?" she asked.
"As soon as I found out he was not mine I hopped on the plane and came right here to you," I replied.
She sat up and looked at me with the saddest eyes.
"Why?" she asked.
That question really hurt me. Did she not know how much I loved her? I only wanted to be with her. I prepared to pour my heart out to her, to tell her how I didn't want to live a day without her. I began,
"Iris, I think you are so amazing. I never wanted to hurt you and I only chose her because of the baby. I want to be with you. I am in love with you, and I don't ever want to spend a day without you."
She stared at me for a long time and then leaned back onto the pillow.
"Your timing is perfect,' she said. I wasn't sure if she was being sarcastic or genuine.
"Are you being serious or sarcastic?"

"I don't know yet."
"Do you love me?"
"I did."
"You did? Meaning you don't anymore?"
"I'm not sure. You really hurt me. You chose her over me. I know why you did it, but it didn't hurt any less."
"I know. I knew that it would hurt you, but I hoped that you would understand that I needed to stand up and do what was right by her."
"I get that but-"
"No buts Iris I love you. We're going to be together and I will worship you in the way that you deserve."
"Ok," she replied sheepishly.
"Ok, now sit up so I can wash your back."

She moved and didn't say a word. I'm glad she agreed. As a lawyer, she was very argumentative. She was also an Alpha woman that needed to feel safe and secure with a man. She always told me that I gave her that. However, I had a nagging feeling that this wasn't over, but I was going to enjoy the moment of her allowing me to take care of her. I finished washing her back and asked if she wanted me to wash the rest of her. She said no and that she wanted to be left alone for a while. I refilled her glass with wine and then showered in the guest bathroom. I was sitting at the foot of the bed when she emerged from the bathroom. She was only wearing a towel. She sat next to me and laid her head on my shoulder. I embraced her. She smelled so good, but I knew sex was out of the question. I just needed to hold and comfort her tonight.

"Are you ready to lie down?" I asked.
 I looked at the clock and it was 2 AM.
"Yes," she said and started to kiss my neck.
Ok! Maybe sex wasn't out of the picture. I picked her up and laid her down on the bed. I began to kiss her all over. I needed to show her how much I really missed her and how much she really meant to me. She opened her legs and motioned for me to enter her.

"Not yet baby," I whispered and put my head there instead. I made sure to please her until she begged me to stop. We then kissed and caressed each other. When I finally entered her she was so moist. It felt so good and she was moaning in my ear. I gave her my all and after she had cum twice I finally finished myself. We laid there sweaty and satisfied. She laid on my chest and went to sleep.

Chapter Two: Back to Business

Colin and I spent the rest of the weekend talking and making love. I told him all about everything that happened between me and Sebastian, and he filled me in on his marriage and what happened with the baby. It was good to have my man back, but most importantly my friend. Maybe I was just lonely and needed to be comforted and he gave me that. He was always the person that I was able to confide in. He gave me great advice, never judged me, and always protected me, even if it was from myself. He was everything I wanted in a partner, but I wasn't too sure that I should just forgive him that easily. He did leave me for her and had no qualms about it. Yet, he seemed so sincere and sorry. He was very attentive and even turned off his phones for the entire day Sunday. He had never done that before, so I took his efforts as being genuine. I was so confused but I was enjoying his efforts of making it up to me all weekend.

Monday morning rolled around very quickly. My alarm went off as I was tangled around Colin's body. My legs were wrapped around his waist and my arm around his neck. I slept on his back, because it brought me comfort. Plus his back really turned me on.
"Baby, are you going to work today?" he asked groggily.
"I have to. I have meetings with new clients today," I replied, rolled over onto my back, and pulled the covers over my head. He put his head under the cover as well and asked, "So are we hiding from Monday?" He was being silly. I laughed,
"Yes, be quiet before it gets us." He laughed and began to lick my left nipple.
"Stop babe. I have to go to work!" I whined.
"Well, I need some beard moisturizer first," he said and positioned himself in between my legs.

"Damn you," I moaned as he began to lick and suck on my clit. I tried to scoot up on the bed, but he quickly pulled me back into him and bit the inside of my thigh.

"Oww," I laughed.

"Stop running from me then," he said from under the covers. I closed my eyes and allowed him to please me in the way he wanted. I was just about to cum when my phone began to ring. I was about to reach for it when he pulled me back to him, but instead of continuing to give me oral he penetrated me very roughly.

"Don't you dare think about answering that phone until I'm done with you," he said as he pinned my arms behind my head with one arm and gripped my waist with the other.

"Fuck!" I exclaimed. After several positions and lots of sweat, we both finished and I could barely move. I was lying on my stomach when he smacked me on my ass and said, "Ok now get up and make the donuts baby."

I laughed and then began to whine. I really wanted to stay in bed with him, but there were new clients that I had to meet and I wanted to make a great first impression.

I took my cell phone into the bathroom and called Sasha back.

"Good Morning my darling," I said when she answered.

"I'm just calling to remind you that you have a very busy day and to take the dick out of your mouth," she said cracking up.

"Girl, I'm getting in the shower and will be on my way soon," I said and laughed right along with her. I quickly showered and got dressed. When I walked back into the bedroom I did not see Colin.

"Babe, where are you?" I yelled out as I walked down the corridor toward the guest bathroom thinking he may be in there. The door was open and the light was turned off. Where could he be? Then I smelled bacon. Was he cooking me breakfast? I walked swiftly to the kitchen not knowing what to expect. He was standing over the stove scrambling eggs in the skillet.

"I wanted to make sure I sent you off to work completely satisfied. I don't want a man with a bacon sandwich stealing my girl," he joked and motioned for me to sit down at the counter.

"Wow! I didn't even know your ass could cook," I said as I picked up a piece of bacon and ate it.

"Wait, when did I even get bacon? I need to go to the grocery store this week," I asked perplexed.

"Oh, I had Amazon Fresh bring us some groceries yesterday while you were sleeping," he said.

"Oh, wow. I didn't even know you did that," I said impressed.

"I'm more than a handsome guy with muscles," he said and flexed his biceps. I laughed.

"No, you are also amazing in bed," I replied kissing him on the arm he just flexed. He fixed me a plate and sat a cup of tea in front of me.

"Ok, don't start spoiling me. I will expect this all the time from you," I said jokingly.

"Baby, you can get breakfast every morning for the rest of your life if you forgive me and allow us to move past this," he said.

"Hmmm, we may be able to make a deal if you make me bacon all the time," I said laughing. He made bacon, scrambled eggs with onions and peppers, raisin toast, and tea.

I looked at my watch. My car was going to pull up in 15 minutes.

"Ok, I need to eat quickly because Greg will be here at 8:30," I said drinking my tea.

"Ok, while you're gone I'm going to contact my lawyer and get a move on this divorce and begin the process of moving here to Chicago," he said. He stared awaiting my reaction.

"Ok," I shrugged not wanting to give him too much.

I was still very apprehensive about this entire thing, but I had to get my mind ready for work. Greg, my driver, sent me a text letting me know that he was pulling up and to bring my umbrella because the forecast predicted rain. I walked toward the door and put on my yellow Hunter boots to match my yellow blazer, grabbed my umbrella and briefcase and opened the door.

"Um, can I get a kiss goodbye?" Colin snapped.

"Sorry baby," I stood on my tiptoes to kiss him.

"Have a good day beautiful," he said kissing me on my forehead. I smiled all the way to the office thinking about our weekend together.

Sasha was already sitting at her desk when I arrived at the office. She handed me a cup of tea and a bagel.

"Thanks, Sasha. Colin made me breakfast this morning too," I said and took the items from her.

"Oh, wow he's laying it on pretty thick isn't he?" she laughed.

"Well he has a lot of making up to do with that dumb shit he pulled," I replied.

"That he does," she said following me into my office.

"So are you ready for the rundown today?" she asked.

"Sure, tell me how busy my day is going to be," I answered sarcastically.

"Well your first client isn't until 9:30 so you have a minute to take a breather, but you go nonstop until 3," she said.

"Did you schedule me a lunch?" I asked.

"You have lunch at the Walnut Room with Dr. Robinson," she said and gave me the side-eye.

"Oh, damn I forgot all about meeting with him. We set that up weeks ago," I said.

I rubbed my temple trying to not become overwhelmed with my day. I usually only scheduled two or three clients a day and used the rest of the time for research and follow-ups. It was springtime though and you know what they say that most people come out of hibernation and begin cheating in the spring. Spring and summertime flings were good for business, so I was happy.

I checked my email and began to sip my tea. My office phone rang and I slid my chair to look at Sasha. She walked into my office mouthing, "I don't know who that is" because all calls should be routed from her.

I answered annoyingly, "This is Iris Sandford, how may I help you?"
"You can help me by returning my phone calls young lady," my dad barked at me.
"Hey, Daddy. I miss you too," I giggled.
"I haven't heard from you in a few days. Are you sure everything is ok?" he asked.
He had this uncanny sense of knowing when I wasn't in the right headspace.
"Yes, Daddy. Colin came back. He found out the baby wasn't his," I blurted out.
"Oh, and how do you feel about that?" he asked, and I could hear him sitting back into his chair.
"Honestly, I'm confused, but I do love him. I'm going to take some time to sort everything out in my head," I sighed.
"Well, trust your gut my Princess. If it doesn't feel right, then it isn't. Use your head because your heart will have you in situations that may require your Daddy to come get you out of," he laughed.
"Whoa there. It will be none of that. I got this Daddy,' I paused, 'and I missed hearing your voice."
"Same here baby girl."
"Oh, guess who I'm having lunch with today?" I asked excitedly.
"Who?" he replied and matched my enthusiasm.
"Dr. Robinson! I can't believe he reached out to me after all of these years. He was one of my favorite professors at Hampton," I rattled on not listening to my dad's heavy breathing.
"Dad? You still there?" I asked because he wasn't responding.
"I'm here baby. I actually need to call you back Princess I love you!"
"I love you too Dad," I replied and he hung up.

I looked at the phone. That was weird. I was usually the one rushing him off the phone, but he hung up on me. I shrugged my shoulders thinking that something came up but made a mental note to ask him about it when we spoke again.

"Are you ready for your first client?" Sasha walked in and asked me.

"Sure, fill me in," I said and motioned her to sit down.

"Let me just give you the rundown of the day so I don't have to do this every time someone comes in," she said.

"Ok, makes sense," I shrugged.

"Your first client is Toni T. Remember her? She's just paying a visit but said she has some juicy gossip for you. I didn't ask."

"Ok," I scratched my head.

"Next is this news anchor for channel 6. She wants to talk about a scandal that may need to be diverted at the station."

"What's her name?" I asked annoyed that she wasn't giving me details.

"Sally Brown," she replied. "Did you read my email and your calendar at all?"

"Actually, I didn't," I responded sheepishly.

That was usually my Sunday night ritual because Sasha was super thorough. "I'm sorry babe, just fill me in."

"Ok, next you have lunch with Dr. Robinson, then a follow-up phone call with the Lowensteins. Lastly, you have a meeting with Sebastian's mother. She is a client-this isn't a friendly visit."

"A client as in she booked me for a service?" I asked confused.

"Yes, she was adamant about being treated as a client and not as a mother-in-law. Her words," Sasha said as she threw up her hands. She must have known I was about to give her a dirty look.

"Ok," I sighed.

"Yeah my thoughts exactly," she stood and walked out of the door.

I sat back in my chair and closed my eyes. It was going to be a long day.

I heard a knock at the door and I knew it was Toni T. I looked at the clock and it was 9:28. She was always very punctual. I mentally prepared myself to deal with whatever fuckery she was about to bring me. I was on a high from my weekend with Colin, but somehow I felt like today's events were going to spoil it.

"Your 9:30 is here," Sasha called and said at exactly 9:30 A.M.

I walked out of my office fixing my blazer.

"Iris girl you always look fierce," Toni exclaimed and ran to give me a hug. She stood about 6'3 and still had the build of a man; however, she really looked like a woman. All of her plastic surgery and weave would make you think she was just a basketball player. She was very feminine in the way she dressed, spoke, and walked.

"Toni, girl you look amazing," I exchanged pleasantries.

"Are you ready for everything I need to tell you?" she asked giggling like a schoolgirl.

"I'm not sure. You always drop a bomb on me," I laughed.

I led the way into the conference room. Toni was wearing a white cat suit with a navy blue blazer and yellow shoes. Her fashion was on point. Her hair was in a high ponytail.

"Girl these few months have been so crazy since I last saw you," she said and sat across from me.

"Oh! I'm sure. Are you hiring me or is this a catch up?"

"A little bit of both,"

"Ok, what's up?"

"So Lowenstein is playing me girl. I think he is cheating on me with another tranny!"

"What?" I asked and tried not to laugh.

"I'm dead ass serious. I think he is cheating on me and I want to catch him up girl!"

"Ok. Tell me the story from the beginning," I said. I was more interested in how she knew what was going on.

"So we were out one night and he left his phone to go and use the restroom. Of course his old ass does not know how to mute notifications so someone kept texting him and sending pictures. The name was Destiny. C'mon now Destiny is either a tranny or a stripper."

"Did you see the pictures?"

"I only saw breast. I didn't see anything else. He came back into the room."

"Wait! I thought you all weren't together. I thought he didn't want to have anything else to do with you after the incident?" She rolled her eyes. "Now you know he can't resist this good shit right here," she said and touched her private parts. "We're together. Always will be."

"I have so many questions Toni, but I will refrain from asking them in this business meeting."

"Girl we are friends. You can ask me anything. I'm an open book," she said and opened her legs.

"Oh! Ok! Well have you completely transitioned?" I asked.

"No, I will keep my penis. I've never wanted a vagina. Plus my men like to be fucked in the ass with all ten inches of this man meat," she said and mimicked a pelvic thrust.

"Oh wow, ok!" I laughed. She laughed too. She had to know that was a little raunchy.

"Ok, so what exactly do you want me to find out and if I'm not mistaken you can't sue him or anything like that due to the terms of your previous agreement," I replied.

"Why can't I?" she whined.

"Do you just want more money?" I asked.

"Yes, but I also don't want another bitch touching what's mine," she replied haughtily.

"He's married Toni. He's not yours," I reprimanded and looked at her with the side eye.

"He's mine. He hasn't touched his wife or any real woman for years. He belongs to me."

"Ok! Ok! What do you want me to do?"

"I want you to find out who Destiny is," she replied.

"You know I can't do that. You know you can't do anything remotely like that. He already put you on the show and gives you nice monthly allowance. You're just being greedy and bratty right now," I said and folded my arms across my chest. There was silence.

"You're right. Damn, I hate that you're right," she moped.

"You know I'm right. Now if Destiny does exist you better investigate like every other woman does and snoop through his phone. Even though I don't recommend that because you aren't about to leave him and leave that money so just let that man be with Destiny and whoever else he wants to be with," I said.
"Ok," she sighed.
She gave me a hug. "We need to do brunch soon. I know this popping spot," she said.
"'I'm always down for some good food and drinks," I said walking her to the door.
"How much do I owe Sasha girl?" she asked and opened her purse.
Sasha looked up at me bewildered.

"Just charge her the consultation fee. She just needed to talk," I stated.
"Thanks darling."
"You're welcome.
"Send me some dates for brunch and I will get back to you."
She sashayed out of the door.

I walked into my office and put my head down on my desk. If this was how the day was going to start then I knew I was in for a crazy one.
I had about thirty minutes until my next client. I decided to check my emails since I was on do not disturb all weekend. It was the usual emails about service inquiries, testimonials, and follow-ups.
I forwarded them all to Sasha and made a mental note to give her my email password so she could check them moving forward. In the beginning I still received personal emails to this account, but now it was all business since this was the email on my website. I shifted through all of the spam, promotions, and primary emails until a subject line caught my eye.

It read: Woman-to-Woman.

I sat back in my chair and closed my eyes. I had to be completely prepared for what I was about to read. It could just be Colin's wife finally emailing about their situation. That was the only logical explanation I could come up with. But how would she know anything about me? I clicked on the email and began to read. My eyes widened as I continued to read the email. It wasn't Colin's wife at all. It was one of Sebastian's background dancers letting me know that she had been having an affair with him for over three years and he had broken it off with her because of me and she wanted to let me know that she was still sleeping with him from time to time. I laughed hysterically.

Obviously I laughed too loudly because Sasha came into my office trying to see what was so funny. I let her read the email and she started to laugh as well.
"Girl this has to be a joke," she remarked.
"Maybe it is," I replied.
I wasn't even going to even reply to it. Sebastian was a player and I've known that since high school. Monogamy wasn't something he was even capable of.
I just wanted to believe that I would be the main chick and the other ones knew their place. They obviously did because this chick went out of her way to email me and make herself known. I knew she was young because an older woman understood her place in a man's life and would never email a man's main chick or wife. This was extremely childish.
"So what are you going to do?" Sasha asked still laughing.
"Absolutely nothing," I responded.
"Yeah this is super crazy. It may not even be real," Sasha said.
"Oh it's real. She knows he has my name tattooed on his back. It's hidden inside of another tattoo so unless she is a deranged fan she is definitely fucking him," I replied.
"Well delete the email and ignore it," Sasha suggested.
"That's exactly what I'm going to do," I stated.

I deleted the email but a part of me was still curious. I knew that Sebastian was a hoe, it kind of came with being the lead singer of a band. Women were always at his disposal and threw themselves at him. On some nights we would laugh at the messages women would send in his DMs. They were raunchy and at times a bit pathetic, but he loved the attention. Always did and always will.

Before I could even gather my thoughts I saw my next client sitting in the lobby. She was a blond and thin news anchor from D.C. Her name was Sally Brown, a very cliché name, but she claimed it was her birth given name. I wondered why she flew all the way from D.C to Chicago to hire me. There were plenty of lawyers and private investigators in that scandalous town.

She wore a tweed blazer and skirt with a neatly buttoned up blouse. She looked like she just stepped out of a Nieman's catalogue. Every inch of her was perfect and meticulous, almost too perfect. I watched her from my desk as Sasha offered her coffee or water. She took a water bottle and shook her red bottomed left foot anxiously. She was early, and I was curious. I closed my office door and she turned around as if I had startled her. She was a bit too jumpy for me.

"Mrs. Brown, do you mind following me into the conference room?" I asked.
"It's just Ms. and sure no problem," she replied and gathered her Gucci briefcase from the seat next to her.

I formally introduced myself and gave her a brief synopsis of my work and background. She nodded in approval and began to shift in her seat, as if she was trying to get comfortable. She cleared her throat and spoke in a very small voice, "I'm about to tell you something that can blow the lid off someone's political candidacy as well as take down a few Senators. I can't trust anyone in Washington and I know you don't have any political ties. I will probably die from giving you this information, but I have to tell someone and it has to be leaked."

"Oh wow," I replied and adjusted myself in my seat. "Continue," I pleaded. She began to tell her story and my jaw dropped. She had evidence that would blow the whistle on an underage prostitution ring and possible sex trafficking that was happening in Washington D.C. It was hard evidence that made my head spin. We sat in silence for a while and she sighed heavily. It was almost as if a weight was being lifted off her shoulders. We sat in silence and stared at each other. I spoke first.

"Wow!" I exclaimed.

"I know this is a lot," she replied.

"It's way more than a lot. This is a mountain of bullshit. I don't even know how you know all of this," I said. I got up and began to pace the room.

"I have a confidant in the Senate who is actually a first hand participant in this sex ring that wants immunity once it comes out," she stated.

"Immunity? For being a damn pedophile?" I asked shocked. "How does that even work?" I asked more to myself not really expecting an answer.

"I don't know, but I think you are the only person that can help me Ms. Sandford."

"I'm sorry, but this is far beyond anything I have ever dealt with in my career. I am not Olivia Pope, and I don't know who gave you the impression that I was," I stated harshly.

"Again, I know this is a lot, but I think you would be able to help me save some young girls lives and put these dirty old men in jail."

Again there was silence.

"I really have to think about this case. People get killed for stories like this. I am not a DC fixer. They have plenty of those. Why don't we just anonymously send this to the press along with all of the evidence you have?" I asked. I sat down feeling a bit dizzy from her story.

"In cases like this they need evidence and first hand accounts. Someone will have to come forward and I don't want it to be me. If you can't help me I don't know who else can. I don't trust anyone in DC and you came highly recommended. Are you afraid?" she asked.

"Being afraid is an understatement," I replied defeated.
I knew that I needed to help. I wanted to help, but was I willing to risk my life and career to break something like this to the public. I was used to cheating husbands and TMZ scandals, not CNN scandals. This was like front page Time magazine worthy.
"Sally. I will have to think about this case. I want to help, I really do, but this is a lot. I will get back to you within 48 hours with a decision. Is that ok?" I asked.
She stood up. "Sure," she said in a quiet voice and started to walk towards the door.

She handed me her card before she walked out of the door.
"My cell number is on the back. I'm staying at the Drake hotel downtown."
"The Drake? People still stay at the Drake?" Sasha asked.
"I guess if you want to hide and be incognito then sure," I replied.
Sally looked at us perplexed.
"Oh, we're just saying there are more popular hotels to stay in Chicago Sally. I haven't heard anyone say they were staying at the Drake for over ten years," I explained.
"Well that's where I will be and I hope it's as obscure as you all think it is."

We watched as she walked out of the door.
"What was that about?" Sasha asked, followed me into my office, and plopped down on the couch. I stood at the window and looked at the women walking their dogs with no cares in the world.
"Um, I guess I don't even want to know," Sasha whispered sarcastically.

"Seriously I don't even know if I can take her on as a client. She really just dropped a bomb on me and I think it's above my capacity to take on," I sat down on my rug with my legs crossed.

"What? Superwoman? The infamous Iris Sandford thinks a case is too big for her? What did she tell you? The President is a pedophile?" Sasha laughed.

"Shit, he may be," I replied.

"Are you joking?"

"Seriously this case could put a lot of politicians in jail and I don't know if I want to be involved in political bullshit like this. It's too much," I whined.

"Oh wow. What did you tell her?" Sasha asked.

"To give me 48 hours and I would tell her my answer. I really don't know what I am going to do. I need to call my Daddy," I whined again.

"Speaking of fathers, your old professor will be here in about 15 minutes for your lunch date."

"Ugh, I forgot about that. Now I don't want to go," I pouted and pretended to throw a tantrum.

"Girl, I'm scared for you. I've never seen you act like this. She must have really dropped a bomb on you?"

"Girl a Hiroshima sized bomb. It's so salacious that I don't even want to tell you for fear of your safety. Luckily I don't have names yet."

"Is this something you can even tell your father?" she asked.

"I can because I don't know any of the details. I can just tell him the overall situation and ask his advice on if it's something I should get involved in. My Daddy never lets me down."

"Daddy's girl!" she laughed.

"All day, every day," I chuckled.

We sat there in silence for a while and I decided to call my father once the lunch date was over. I also made a mental note to ask him about how he rushed me off the phone earlier.

Dr. Robinson arrived five minutes early to our lunch date. I was excited to see him. He was my favorite professor at Hampton. He taught Biology when I wanted to be premed and it was because of him that I realized I wanted to become a lawyer.

"Iris, you don't look a day over 21," he exclaimed.

"Thank you, Dr. Robinson. You look good yourself," I replied as we embraced.

Dr. Robinson stood about 5'10 with a slim build. His salt and pepper hair and beard was becoming and he looked good for his age. He could definitely be somebody's sugar daddy. We decided to walk down the street to Giordano's, which is infamous for its pizza instead of taking a cab to the Walnut Room. Giordano's had the best pizza. The rain had stopped and it was a nice spring day. We decided to sit outside and enjoy the weather. We caught up on current happenings at Hampton and other small talk. We talked about Bryant and his team being in the playoffs. He was excited that we remained friends because we were once lost teenagers on a huge college campus. We ate our deep-dish pizzas and drank Coronas while we reminisced.
"So what are you doing in Chicago?" I asked.
"I'm here to do a guest lecture at the University of Chicago," he replied.
"Oh, that's nice and you just decided to look me up for lunch?" I asked.
"You were one of my favorite students," he said and picked up another slice.
"Only because I stayed in your office for fear of failing Bio. It was because of you that I decided to become a lawyer. I love science, but that class was so hard," I whined.

"You just had some skill gaps, but you were very tenacious. Being a lawyer suits you though. I'm proud of you."
"Awww, thank you," I said proudly.
"What else do you want to do while you're in town?" I asked.
"Well, although this is a business trip, it's also something important I need to take care of," he said, wiped his mouth and sat up straight. His tone became really serious and it made me sit up in my seat.

"What's so serious?" I asked intrigued by his change in behavior. I was thinking that he needed to hire me for some reason.

The last thing I wanted was to delve into his secrets. There are some things I didn't want to know about certain people.

"Well actually there is something we need to talk about," he said.

Here we go I thought to myself.

"Sure. Do you need to hire me for something?" I asked.

"Not actually. There is something I need to discuss with you," he stated.

"Sure. I'm all ears," I replied. I repositioned myself to give him my full attention.

"This is actually kind of hard to tell you, but I'm going to come right and just say it," he started then there was a long pause. I was getting anxious to hear this news.

"I think I'm your father," he blurted.

"What?" I laughed.

I was still laughing and he sat there looking at me defeated.

"Iris, I'm serious. Your mother and I had an affair and I think I'm your father," he said solemnly.

"Wait! Are you serious right now?" I asked. I slumped in my chair. He pulled out an old letter and gave it to me. I read as he continued to talk.

"Yes! I've known your mother for a long time. She is actually the love of my life. You act so much like me that I really think it's true. Your mother has denied it for so long that I want to know the truth. I need to know," he stated.

"Wait! What?" I was shocked. My head was spinning. I didn't know what to say. I just sat there and listened to his story about him and my mom's affair.

"Does my Daddy know this?" I asked and reached for my phone to call him.

He was silent. I put the phone down. Now I was really taken aback.

"So my Daddy knows this and didn't tell me?" I exclaimed assuming that my Daddy knew.

"Listen Iris. I just want you to agree to take a DNA test with me, that's all. I don't mean to cause you any trouble or pain, but I'm sure you'd like to know if I'm your father as well."

"I have a father. He's been amazing and always will be," I retorted.
"I know. I get it. Just please agree to think about it. Please," he pleaded.

I sat there dumbfounded. I didn't know what to do or say. I was stunned.
Flabbergasted.
The waiter came and brought the check. He took out his card and paid the bill. I stared at him for a while trying to read him and he stared back.

Was he really my father?

Chapter Three: Loose Ends

The last few days with Iris were amazing. I really wanted to show her how sorry I was and that I needed her. The old adage, "You never know what you got until it's gone," was definitely true in this sense. I thought about her everyday even when things were going well between me and Carmen. She was always on my mind because I knew that deep down I needed to be with her. I would never have verbalized that, but I knew she was the one when I first laid eyes on her. Now that I had her I didn't want to lose her, even if that meant making a complete fool out of myself and being her errand boy, doing her laundry, cooking for her, and making her smile. All things I would have never done for any other woman. I had all of these thoughts as I stood in line to pick up groceries to cook for her tonight. I was going to make her lasagna and try to talk to her about the process I was making with settling my affairs in Miami. I wanted her to know I was serious about moving to Chicago and building a life with her. I even online shopped for wedding rings and had an appointment in the Diamond district to build her the perfect engagement ring.

There was a woman with an infant in a stroller in front of me. I couldn't help but think about CJ and wonder how he was. I had grown attached to him in those past four months. I was excited to be a father and wondered if Carmen would allow me to remain in his life. The baby dropped her toy and I picked it up. At that moment my heart sank. Was I wrong for just leaving the way I did? I abruptly left and fled to Iris. Carmen was wrong, but did she deserve me leaving like that?
"Thank you," the mother replied. Her words snapped me out of my thoughts.
"Oh no problem. You have a beautiful daughter," I replied.
She smiled and went to pay for her groceries. My heart sank so I called Carmen just to check on her.
"Hey Colin," she answered somberly.
"Hey how is CJ?" I asked.

"He's feeding right now. He's doing well."
"Can I Face time you so I can see him?" I asked.
"Sure," she replied.

I pressed the button and didn't expect to see her looking the way she did. Her hair was disheveled, she had on a bathrobe, and it was obvious that she had been crying. She was a model and prided herself on her appearance. I never saw her without makeup, even when we were married. Seeing her like this was disheartening. She was nursing him but stopped to show me his face.
"Hey little man," I said relieved to see him looking healthy. The surgery and blood transfusion had only happened a few weeks before I left. He turned as if he knew my voice. Maybe he did. He smiled and then whined to continue nursing.
"He looks good," I said.
"Yeah, he definitely has his appetite back. He eats so much," she chuckled.
"That's good. How are you?" I asked more out of a formality.
"I mean I know I fucked up and I hate myself for it," she began to cry.
"Hey, let's not go into that. It's over and done with," I replied not really knowing what to say.
"When are you coming home?" she asked.
"Coming home?" I repeated. Was she crazy?
"Yeah, I know you were about to start closing on that outlet mall. You don't have to be here for work?" she asked drying her tears.
"You know I can work from anywhere and that deal is still happening."
"Where are you?" she whined.
I sighed. Was she really about to ask me all of these questions. Calling her was becoming a bad idea.
"It doesn't matter where I am Carmen. Do you need anything? You still have access to the accounts so you shouldn't," I scoffed.
"No. We're fine. Thanks for not cutting me off," she said sarcastically.

"Hey you can stay in the house for as long as you need to. I want you and CJ to be ok," I replied not acknowledging the sarcasm in her voice.
"I appreciate that. I really do," she said trying to sound sincere.
"Ok, well I have to go. I'll reach out to you soon." I hung up the phone before she was able to reply.

I proceeded checking out my groceries with my mind in frenzy. I was beginning to second-guess my hasty decision to just jump on the plane and come to Iris. I didn't even think about how my actions would affect Carmen. Should I have though? I mean CJ wasn't mine and that was the only basis of our marriage and she understood that. It wasn't like we got married because we were in love. I wanted to do right by her and I was raised that a man takes care of his responsibilities. My father instilled that in me before his death. I really thought I was doing the right thing and was prepared to do whatever it took to make sure that my son was being raised by two loving parents. My son. My son. I repeated to myself. But he wasn't my son. I had to remember that.

I loaded the groceries into the truck and decided to give my lawyer a call. I had to make this official, but also make sure that Carmen and CJ would be ok without me.

"Hey my favorite client," he exclaimed when he picked up.
"That's only because I pay you a lot of money," I chuckled.
"What can I do for you today?" he asked.
"I need to get a divorce." I replied.
"Um what? I just drew up the prenup papers!" he exclaimed.
"I know but the baby isn't mine," I replied somberly.
"Oh damn, that's fucked up," he sighed. There was a long silence. "How did you find out?" he firmly asked.

I went through the long story of the surgery and test results. He listened intently. When I was done there was a silence. I could tell he was processing and honestly so was I. I hadn't told anyone the story from beginning to end, not even Iris. I just told her he wasn't mine and how I found out. I left out the details about the argument we had for weeks leading up to me leaving.

"Damn, man, that's some heavy shit. Like some movie shit," he finally replied.

"I know right. I can't believe it myself," I said sinking into the seat of the car. I sighed.

"So what do you want me to draw up? You want to give her a settlement or something? You know she signed the prenup so she can't walk away with much."

"I know but I want to make sure they are ok. Can we start a trust fund for him and give her a monthly allowance?"

"You sure you want to do that?" he asked shocked.

"I don't want them just out there. You know she doesn't have a job," I replied.

"Is that even your concern? Where is she now?" he asked.

"She's in the house in Miami."

"Where are you?"

"Chicago," I responded.

"Whoa! Why are you in Chicago?"

"That's another story but I may relocate here."

"Ok this is too much. I want you to think about everything and give me a call in a few days. Do you need me to go and check on them?" he asked.

"You can, I just talked to her but immediately regretted the call," I sighed.

"Ok. I will check on them before the week is over and give you a call back," he said and hung up.

I just sat there, head spinning. I needed to get some advice from Iris, but was afraid of how she would react. The last thing I needed was her in her feelings about this.

I started the car and headed toward the house. I unloaded the car and headed to the kitchen. I could hear sniffling coming from the bedroom.

"Iris," I called out.

She didn't respond and the sniffles turned into wails. I immediately dropped the groceries and ran to her.

"What's wrong babe?" I asked concerned as to why she was crying and at home so early.

"I---I---I--just---can't------deal-----with-----all---of this," she cried.

"All of what?" I asked trying to comfort her. She buried herself in my chest and continued to cry. I just held her. I had no idea why she was crying. She held her phone in her hand.

"Can I see your phone? I asked knowing it would recover the reason for her tears. She handed it to me without hesitation. I looked through it and saw that there were twelve missed calls from her father and a few from her mother. Ok. This was a family thing. But why was she crying? Her parents were her world, especially her dad. She turned and positioned herself in the fetal position with her back facing me. I tried to spoon her, but she was curled up so tight. I just rubbed her booty hoping to soothe her.

A text came in from Sasha.

Sasha: Iris, are you ok? Your parents keep calling the office. Please call me back. I'm worried about you.

Me: This is Colin. What happened?

Sasha: I don't know. She went to lunch with an old professor and came back crying. She ran out without saying a word.

Me: I think she is asleep now. Maybe we should call B.

Sasha: That's a good idea. Hold please.

I continued to rub on Iris until Sasha sent a reply text

Sasha: B said that he called her father and he wouldn't tell him what happened. Just said to have Iris call him as soon as she wakes up.

Me: Wow. Ok! I wonder what's going on.

I began to pace the floor. It didn't like to see my baby so distraught. She cried herself to sleep and I still didn't know why. I wanted to call her father myself because why would he make her cry? I didn't because he didn't know me and I didn't want to overstep my boundaries with her. The last thing I needed was for her to be upset with me for making the situation worse. I just watched her sleep. She looked so peaceful even though there were tear stains on her cheeks. I kissed her forehead and she rolled over onto her stomach. I didn't want to interrupt her so I went into the kitchen and began to cook. If she wasn't hungry when she woke up then I knew she would be hungry eventually. I wanted to make sure that at least her basic needs were met and that I could provide some comfort for her.

It was after 5PM when I finished cooking. I cooked lasagna and garlic bread. I ate, cleared the dishes, and went to check on Iris. She was still sleeping peacefully so I decided to do some work, check some emails, and watch a baseball game. It was early June, still spring and not quite summer. Chicago didn't really get hot until July still I opened the window and enjoyed the breeze. The baseball game was really just background noise. I poured myself a drink and sat on the couch. I started to thumb through my text messages-there were over a hundred of them from clients, friends, and others in Miami. I had literally cut my world off and ran to Iris. I wasn't on any type of social media, so this was the only way to keep up with the people who loved me. The group chat with my fraternity brothers had over 300 messages. There was no way I was going to read them all so I just called Scott who I was very close to.
"Hey frat, how's it going?" I said when he answered the phone.
"Where the fuck have you been?" he yelled in the phone.
"In Chicago, I will have to tell you that story but catch me up on these thousands of texts we have," I said.
"Chicago?" Never mind. We were just trying to plan our annual island vacation and since you're the one with the chopper and all the connects we were trying to see what have up your sleeve."

"Shit, it is almost July. Fuck! I haven't even thought about that damn vacation. I will start planning it now. What islands ya'll thinking about?" I asked opened my laptop and began an email to my travel agent. She handled all of our vacations. We had been island hopping for the past ten years, but going on yearly vacations since we crossed. It was also our twentieth year so we had planned on doing it big.
"Man, they've been going back and forth between Aruba, Turks & Caicos, and Bermuda," he replied.
"Ok, I'm emailing Amber right now and giving her the options. I will tell her that we will need something tomorrow and I will share it with the group."
"Ok are you really ok?" he asked.
"Man, it's a lot going on, but I will be ok," I sighed.
"I'll actually be in Chicago next week at this convention. We need to link up. It's some shit I need to talk to you about too," he said.
"Ok bet. Send me the dates and we will definitely make it happen. You can come over for dinner, I replied.
"Dinner? Nigga where you at? An Air B&B?" he chuckled.
"Nah, I'm staying with my lady and future wife fool," I retorted.
"Future wife? Where is Carmen?" he asked.
"Long story man, long story," I sighed.
"Wow ok. Can't wait to hear this shit. I gotta go though, the kids are getting out of practice," he said.
"Alright one," I said and waited for his response, "One," he replied. We hung up the phone.

I sat on the couch for a minute thinking about previous vacations and the trouble we got into. There was always the inevitable threat of jail time and someone coming up missing due to drunkenness. It was always a good time reconnecting with my friends and catching up.

I was deep in thought when I heard a phone ring. I totally forgot that I turned on Iris' ringer while she was asleep. I hurried to the room so the phone wouldn't wake her.

She tussled with the cover trying to search for the phone. It was on the nightstand. I was about to turn it off, but noticed her father was calling again. I ignored the call and powered it off. I tried to tiptoe out of the room when she called my name, "Colin, come back and hold me," she whined.

"Of course Baby girl," I said climbed into bed and spooned her.
"No, turn over," she whined.
I turned onto my back and she climbed on top of me. We slept like this from time to time and I loved to feel her body on top of mine. She snuggled into my neck and I rubbed her back.
"You ready to tell me what's wrong?" I asked.
"No, just hold me. I want to go back to sleep," she whispered.

I didn't respond. I just held her and let her cry. I hated this feeling of not knowing what was going on and also not being able to fix her problems. We were always able to talk things out and bounce ideas off of each other. There were many times that she was the only person who understood where I was coming from and vice versa. Whatever was bothering her was taking a toll on her spirit and I did not like it. An hour passed and I could tell that she was struggling with sleep.

"Colin, can you go make me a drink? A really strong one?" she asked as she headed to the bathroom.
"Sure baby," I obliged knowing to just pour some whiskey in a glass with a few ice cubes.
I found her bottle of Buffalo Trace whiskey and added two ice cubes. She was sitting on the side of the bed with her head in her hands as I handed her the glass. She took a few gulps and then handed the glass back to me.
"Can I have another one?" she asked softly.
"Sure, but only one more unless you're calling off tomorrow," I reprimanded.
"I am. I need to unplug," she exhaled and then fell back into the bed, pulling the covers over her head. I laughed and went to fix her another drink.
 "It can't be that bad," I said and her the second drink.
 "Oh but it is," she screamed.

I was baffled. I had never seen her so distraught and upset before. She was usually very poised. Being frazzled was not her thing. She drank the second drink rather fast too. I joked and asked her if she wanted some water. She shot me a dirty look and handed me the glass. I took it but instead brought her a bottle of Riesling. She needed to lay off the whiskey. I didn't bother with a glass just put a straw in the bottle. She chuckled and took the bottle from me and began to sip it.
"You just gave me a straw huh?" she laughed.
"You don't need a glass, just finish the whole bottle," I retorted. She sighed and continued drinking out of the straw. I turned on the TV, sat at the edge of the bed, and started watching Forensic Files. She belched and then got back under the cover. About 10 minutes into the episode she started to breathe heavy. I turned my head and she was sleeping peacefully. I guess two glasses of whiskey and an entire bottle of wine relaxed her enough to welcome sleep again. I smiled watching her sleep. I still had no idea what she was going through, but I would be there when she woke up to comfort her.

Chapter Four: Twenty-Four Hours

"Where the fuck you been? I haven't heard from you all day!" he screamed through the phone. "What if something had happened to you? You could have been kidnapped or laying in a ditch somewhere for all I know!" I laughed.
I couldn't help it, I kept laughing.
"It's not fucking funny Sasha," he screamed, that made me laugh even harder.
"Open the fucking door," he screamed and hung up. I opened the door trying to hold in my laughter. He immediately put his hand around my neck and backed me into the wall.
"When I fucking call you, you need to answer the fucking phone," he said and then kissed me.
"I missed you too babe," I said and rubbed his back.
We kissed passionately with his hand still around my neck. He tried to stop but I raised my leg and pulled him back to me with my foot. I didn't want to lose the rhythm of the kiss.
"Damn, don't start something you can't finish," he whispered in between kisses.
"Oh you know I can," I whispered back.
He tightened his grip around my neck making my panties wet. He knew exactly what to do to make me crave him.

"Get your bag so you can come to my house," he commanded. I left him standing in the hall and went to my room to pack a bag. I know he didn't want to stay in my apartment because of my roommate, although she was hardly ever home. He didn't follow me into the room because we both knew we would never leave.

There was a car waiting for us downstairs. We sat in the backseat and I laid my head on his shoulder. We didn't say anything just held hands and listened to the radio. When we finally made it to his penthouse he led me to the balcony. There was wine and food set up with candles and music.
"Aww, you had this planned?" I asked.
"I did. I'm still mad at you though," he replied. I laughed again.

We ate and drank an entire bottle of wine in silence. I knew he was deep in his thoughts and so was I. The view from his penthouse was breathtaking and I stood there just appreciating the beautiful skyline. He stood behind me and began to kiss on my neck.

Kissing turned into fondling, which turned into me, leading him into the bedroom and undressing for him. He always stared at me as if I was the most beautiful woman in the world. I had on an oversized black t-shirt, red lace panties, and knee high socks. Stripping down naked for him was always a treat because I loved the way he made me feel. I kept the socks on but slowly removed everything.

"Come here," he motioned for me to sit on his lap.
I straddled him and he kissed my neck. He slowly made his way to my breasts while palming my ass. I began to grind on him slowly as he licked and sucked on my nipples. A moan of ecstasy escaped from my lips. I threw my head back and placed my hands on his knees to keep my balance. He continued to lick and suck until I begged him to fuck me.
"Please, please," I kept saying.
He laughed, picked me up, and threw me on the bed. He took my socks off and I groaned. I hated being in bed without socks. He put on some music and left out of the room. He came back after a few seconds and told me to stand up. I obliged.
"Turn around," he said.
I did so slowly. He then placed a blindfold on my face.
"Oh, what is this?" I asked.
"Shhh just relax," he whispered.
He pushed me onto the bed. I was on my stomach.

"Put your ass up," he commanded.
I did as I was told.

"No, arch your back," he said pushing my back down.
I was forced into the position he wanted me in. I then felt his tongue inside of me and I squealed. He devoured me and left me moaning and panting. I came three times and collapsed onto the bed.

"I'm not done with you yet," he said and positioned me back into doggy style. He then entered me slowly. We both let out moans. Him inside of me was so fulfilling. He gave me long and slow strokes, teasing me until I regained my composure.

"Damn girl," he moaned. I continued to throw it back until he couldn't take it anymore.
"Damn, you're about to make me cum," he groaned and held onto me until we both collapsed. I don't even remember falling asleep, just waking up to the sun beaming on my face.

I was about to get up until I felt him pressing against me and kissing my neck.
"Good morning beautiful," he said as he rubbed my breasts and started to grind on my butt.
"B, again?" I laughed.
 "I can't get enough of your sexy ass," he said and flipped me over and entered me slowly.
Morning sex was always good because I stayed moist from the night before. I wrapped my legs around his waist and pulled him closer. After about twenty minutes of him doing his thing. I began to grind him from the bottom and lick his earlobe.

"Sasha, baby, don't do that to me right now," he moaned.
I knew that would send him into orbit every time.
I began to grind harder. He placed his hands under my ass making the angle hit my clit perfectly. We simultaneously climaxed and just laid there for a while
.

"Ok, get your heavy ass off of me," I screamed as he put his entire body weight on me.

He was a basketball player, tall and muscular, and my small ass was swallowed up by him. He laughed and rolled onto the other side of the bed. I got up to use the bathroom and stumbled a bit when I walked. He laughed. I gave him the middle finger. He told me that he liked to watch me walk after sex because it always took me a minute to get my legs together. I laughed to myself as I stepped into the shower.

"What's so funny?" he asked and pulled back the curtain.
"Damn, you really don't believe in personal space do you?" I asked annoyed.

"I was just all up in you what do you mean personal space?" he asked sincerely.
I just shook my head. He closed the shower curtain and began to brush his teeth while I showered. We traded places and then sat on the bed in towels.
"Are you hungry?" He began to ask but said never mind, took his phone, and went into the other room.

I sat there wondering if he was about to order me some food or call his girlfriend. Throughout the night she called several times and he ignored her calls. I didn't ask questions I didn't want to know the answers to. I got dressed and turned on the news. I checked my phone to see if Iris had called. She hadn't. I was beginning to worry. I had never seen her cry and whatever happened at her lunch threw her into a frenzy. She wouldn't explain anything to me just ran out of the door and told me she would call me later.

B walked back into the room with his phone in his hand, towel still tied around his waist. He was so fucking sexy. He looked up at me and smiled.
"The food will be here in thirty minutes," he said and stood in front of me purposely.
"Stop playing and put some clothes on," I said and slapped him on his rock hard abs.

"We're not putting on clothes today," he said in a serious tone.
"What?" I asked.
"Take those clothes off and get your ass back in bed," he commanded.
"I have to go to work," I pleaded.
"No you don't. I talked to Colin and Iris is closing the Firm for the rest of the week so you can relax and get naked," he said and tickled me.
"What's wrong with Iris?" I asked as I took off my shirt.
"I don't know but Colin told me to call her father because he has blowing up her phone apparently."
"She ran out of the office right after her lunch with her old professor. I could tell she had been crying, but she wouldn't talk to me," I told him taking off my pants.
"Yeah Colin said she has been in and out of sleep, won't eat, and won't talk. I'm worried about her," he said as he stood in front of me again.
"Me too. Whatever they met about took her completely off of her square," I said completely naked now.
'Yeah, I'm really worried. I will call her later, but right now I want to stay in bed with you," he said and pushed me onto the bed.
We cuddled for a while with me on his chest just listening to his heartbeat. He played in my hair while I rubbed his chest.

"Are you ready for the big game?" I asked. The Beasts were in the playoffs and tomorrow was Game 6. If they win tomorrow they will be the NBA Champions.
"I was born ready," he chuckled.
"No, for real are you ready for the big game? I know it's your first time in the finals." I sat up to look him in his eyes. I needed to see his response.
"Real talk, I'm so nervous. That's why I'm here with you. You always make me feel calm, like at home and at peace with you."
He pulled my face to him and kissed me on the forehead.
"Aww, really? I feel the same way about you," I replied.
"Yeah who would have known all of those times you annoyed me would have us laid up like this." He laughed and flipped me over so he was on top of me.

"I love you Sasha," he whispered.
"Really? I asked.
I was more shocked than anything. We had only been together for a few months, plus he had a girlfriend or whatever she was to him.
"I'm being serious. You've gotten me through some tough shit. I appreciate you and yes I do love you. I'm in love with you," he repeated and kissed me on my forehead again.
"I love you too Bryant," I said and kissed him on the lips. There was a knock at the door.

"Foods here!" he exclaimed. He put on a robe and went to the door. I found one of his t-shirts, which looked like a dress on me and met him in the kitchen.
"I was bringing the food to you crazy," he said when I walked into the kitchen.
"It's ok. We can eat at the table," I said and grabbed two glasses from the cabinet and pouring us some orange juice.

"You know you're going to have to let me take care of you when we get married," he said. I almost choked on my juice.
"Married?" I asked.
"Yeah, you know you're gonna be my wife," he grinned.
"Stop playing, B. You know you don't want to get married," I said and hit him on the shoulder.
"When did I ever say that?" he asked. His tone changed. He was serious now.
"I don't know. Just never thought you wanted to get married or have kids or any of that stuff."
"Well now you know I want all of that stuff,' he said.
I didn't reply. Just ate and looked up at him from time to time. He was staring at me every time I looked up at him.
"What?" I asked as I saw him smiling at me.
"You're so beautiful," he said.
"Thank you. You're fine as hell yourself," I replied.
He laughed.
"Well I have to be at practice in about three hours," he said and looked at his watch.

"What are we gonna do to kill time?" I asked slyly and sat on top of the counter in front of him.
"Well I guess I'm not done eating yet," he laughed and opened my robe.

Sex lasted for at least two hours and the last hour he spent in the shower and in his office. I spent the hour checking emails, rescheduling clients, and sending out invoices. I was at work even in B's bed naked. He came back into the room fully dressed and I got up to find my clothes.

"What are you doing?" he asked and looked at my puzzled. I was frantically searching for my underwear.
"I'm trying to get dressed so I can leave with you," I replied.
"Woman, if you don't get back in that bed and wait until I get home. You aren't going anywhere," he said firmly.
"What? I need to go home," I stood back up after he had pushed me into the bed.
"No you don't. I sent your clothes to the cleaners and I ordered you some new underwear. You can chill until I get back," he replied and pushed me back into the bed.
"Ok, Ok," I laughed and pulled the covers over my head.
"Good, now stay naked and right there until I get back," he said wagging his finger at me.
"Can I take a bath?" I asked trying to be funny.
He stood there looking at me for a while.
"No, I'll give you a bath when I get back," he said and walked out of the door.
I laughed out loud. He was so funny. I fell asleep watching a movie on TV.

My phone woke me up. It was Iris.
"Boss lady! OMG! What's going on?"
"Hey Sasha. Everything is going. I was just calling to make sure you knew I was going to take the week off," said softly.

"Yes, I handled everything and no one will call you with Firm business until I give the green light," I responded.

There was silence and I could hear that she was trying to hold back tears. I hated that I didn't know what was going on, but I didn't want to push the issue.

"Iris, you know you can tell me anything. I'm not trying to force you to tell me what's going on, so when you're ready, I'm here for you. I just hope you know that people love you and you don't have to deal with things on your own," I said to her. I wanted to reassure her of our friendship. She wasn't just my boss.

She was still silent. I listened to her breathing become heavy as if she was trying to muster up the strength to tell me what was bothering her. She finally replied in the smallest voice ever, "I know Sasha. I'm trying to wrap my head around all of this and when I'm ready to talk I will call you for sure."

"Ok boss lady. I love you. I'm here and let me know if you need me to do anything else," I replied.

"Thanks." She hung up.

I threw the covers back over my head and sighed. I really wanted to know what took her off of her square so much. I'm glad Colin was there. He would make sure that she was at least eating and taking care of her basic needs. She tended to go into seclusion when she was in her head, luckily he wouldn't let her stay there that long.

B sent a text saying he would be home soon. It was almost 10PM. I wanted to make sure he had food when he got home. I went into the kitchen to see what was in his fridge. It was all water and veggies. I wondered if I could make him a stir-fry but there wasn't any type of rice In hIs cupboards. He opened the door as I was rummaging through the cabinets.

"I thought I told you to stay in bed," he said and placed bags of food on the counter.

"I was going to cook dinner for you, but you don't have food," I replied.

"I do. It's just not the food you want to eat," he snickered.

"I bought us some salmon Caesar salad and dessert," he said and laid the food on the counter.

"Don't you need to eat for your game tomorrow?" I asked questioning why he was eating so lightly.

"That's why I'm not eating a lot. On game days I eat a light breakfast and then do smoothies and protein shakes, but I don't eat that much," he said and stuffed some salad in his mouth.

"Well that explains the fridge full of veggies," I said and joined him eating. We ate in silence, which was odd. I could tell that he was thinking, but didn't want to say anything. His phone rang.

He excused himself and went into the other room. I cleaned up our dishes and poured some more wine for me and some seltzer water for him. I knew he definitely didn't drink before a big game. I headed back into the room when I heard him call my name.

He was in the master bathroom running me a bath. There were candles lit and music playing. I stood there in awe. Who was this man?

"I told you I was going to bathe you when I got home," he said and motioned me to come closer.

He took the glasses from me, took off my t-shirt, and placed me into the tub. It was just the right temperature. I relaxed and closed my eyes. I could get used to the pampering. I felt him get in the tub too. "You know I've lived here for three years and never even wanted to take a bath with somebody," he said and threw bubbles in my face.

"That's good to know I'm special," I giggled.

"Can I tell you a secret?" he asked.

"Sure, hit me with it," I said leaning into him to listen intently.

"I've never even let anyone into my master bedroom. I usually sleep with women in one of the other rooms. Other than Iris, you're the only woman who has slept in my real bed," he said and brushed my hair from my face.

"Aww you really like me huh?" I asked and laid my back against his chest. The tub was massive. Two more people could have fit in there with us. I always wanted to take a bath in his tub from the first time I helped him and Iris pick out his apartment. It was my dream bathroom.

"I do baby girl, I really do,' he replied and wrapped his arms around my torso. We sat in silence. I could feel his heart beating on my back. Then I felt his dick getting hard.
"B!" I exclaimed.
"Ok, get off of me. I can't have sex twenty four hours before this game," he said annoyed.
"Oh, so you want me to go home?" I asked.
He squeezed me.
"No! You're my good luck charm. Have you noticed that I had you stay over before every home playoff game?"
"You did," I said, realizing he was right.
He moved my hair from my neck, kissed it, and squeezed my nipples.
"B! Didn't you say we couldn't do anything?" I whined.
"I said I couldn't have sex, but that has nothing to do with my pleasing you," he said and moved his fingers in and out of me under the water.
"That's not fair," I moaned.
"It's so fair," he said continuing to kiss me.
"No B! Stop! I can wait until you win tomorrow. I will even do your diet with you," I said and turned to kiss him.
"Ok, I really wanted to taste you after you got out of this tub, but we can just continue another day," he said.
I kissed him again and just laid in his arms. The water felt so good I didn't want to get out. He held me for a while and we listened to the smooth jazz that was playing from the speakers. It was such a relaxing and romantic moment.
He started to hum along to the words and caress my arms.

"Do you really love me B?" I asked.
I was hesitant because I didn't know what he was going to say.

"I do. I love you with every fiber of my being," he whispered in my ear.

"So what about your girlfriend?" I asked.
"For real. She is no one. Who am I here with right now?" he said as he rubbed my shoulders.
"That's so much game B. You don't have to do that with me. If you really love me she would be irrelevant," I said sternly.
"You're absolutely right and since it bothers you I will make sure that she is no longer around," he said reassuringly.
"I know you have the ultimate game tomorrow. Let's just enjoy the moment. I don't want you worrying about me and my feelings. You need to focus on winning this championship babe," I said excitedly.

"That's why I love you," he kissed the back of my neck.
"I know! Now let's get out of this tub before we turn into prunes," I laughed.
He helped me out of the tub and wrapped me in a towel like a baby. He carried me into the bedroom and laid me on the bed before rubbing me down with baby oil and putting me under the cover.
"You are so silly!" I exclaimed as he tried to tuck me in.
"Are you ok now?" he asked.
"When was I ever not ok?"
He didn't respond, just laid down behind me and held me. Soon he was asleep and snoring.

This was the best feeling in the world and I hope that he wasn't lying to me about getting married. I could definitely see myself marrying him, having his babies, and loving on him for the rest of our lives. I started to think about our future together before I joined him in dreamland.

Chapter Five: We are the Champions!!!

The Chicago Beasts were the 2019 NBA Champions!!! The city was in an uproar and I couldn't have been prouder of Bryant. His penthouse was full of people. There was music, food, and of course bottles popping everywhere. The game was playing on the big flat screen and he was standing around with some of his teammates talking through the highlights. When B made the game buzzer dunk they all got loud and went nuts. Crazy to think that earlier that morning we were standing in the kitchen dancing and making smoothies. I smiled thinking about how he kissed me and pinned me against the fridge. He said I was his good luck charm, and that he had to have me stay with him the night before each game. Sure enough when that happened he would win. Now I was surrounded by strangers.

I surveyed the room suspecting that it would be full of groupies. The wives and girlfriends of the players were sitting in the formal dining area with each other while everyone else was all over the place. I studied them wondering if I would ever be able to fit in with them, but quickly tossed that thought to the side when B's girlfriend walked over and hugged one of the player's wives. It was obvious that she fits in with that group and knew them. To everyone, she was still his girlfriend and it didn't matter what I was to him or did for him. My anger was starting to boil. I walked towards the door ready to leave. Luckily, Iris and Colin walked in the door just in the nick of time.

"Hey Sasha," she said and hugged me tightly.

"Hey boo, I'm glad you all came. I don't know anyone here," I replied.
"You should have just rode with us from the game. I told you we just had to stop at the house first."
"Yeah, I should have."

Colin came and hugged me. He always smelled so good. I was so happy that he came to his senses and chose Iris, but how ironic that I now found myself in that same situation. Yes, B had a girlfriend. Even during that Marisol bullshit she was there. Her name was Briana, and they had been on and off again for a few years. She was around playing hostess and hanging onto his arm. I tried to pretend that it didn't bother me, but it did. I wanted to sling her ass into a wall every time she kissed him, or laughed her fake ass laugh. I kept telling myself that he didn't really love her that he really loved me, but my emotions were all out of whack.

"Sasha Boo," I heard and turned around. It was my home girl Tanji. I'm glad she came. She was the only one that knew about B and me.
"Hey girl, I'm so glad you're here," I said and hugged her.
"Is that her?" she asked.
"Yes, that's her fake Barbie ass."
"I mean she's cute, but she ain't all that."

Briana stood about 5'7. She was very slim and built like a model. She wore a short pixie cut and had on red mini bodycon dress.

"Exactly," I responded trying not to stare in her direction. Then I looked up and B was staring at me from across the room. Our eyes met and he started to walk toward us. My heart rate quickened and I couldn't help but smile. He hugged Tanji and told her to make herself at home. He then stood behind me and whispered in my ear "Why are you so damn sexy baby?"
I smiled and Tanji walked away.
"Are you having a good time?" he asked and handed me his cup.

"What's in here?" I asked.
"Stop asking questions and just drink it."
I took a sip of the secret concoction. It was actually pretty good.
"Well now I guess I have to get my own cup."
"Yes, but you can fill this one up too," I said, guzzled the rest and handed the cup back to him.
"Ok, I will be right back."

I watched him glide across the room like a god. His body was so amazing. I loved to trace his chest with my fingers and have his arms wrapped around me. Everything about him made my knees quiver.
"When did I fucking fall in love with B's ass?" I asked myself.

Before he could make it to the kitchen, his girlfriend pulled him into a kiss in the middle of the room, in front of everyone. I turned my back because I could no longer watch the spectacle. He told me yesterday that he would make sure that she was no longer in the picture, and although I knew it wouldn't be an overnight fix I kind of hoped that he would tell her not to show up. Now I was feeling all of the emotions of a side chick-jealous, but knowing that there was nothing that I could really do about it at the moment. I wanted to slap her ass and then slap him for making me feel like a fool.
I remember Iris telling me about this same situation with Colin in Miami, and now I knew how she felt. I was angry but knew I didn't have the right to be. No matter what, she was still his girlfriend to the public eye.

I made my way to the bathroom to give myself a pep talk. I was hurting my own feelings plus I didn't want to show anyone that I was annoyed. Someone came out of the guest bathroom just as I walked up. I quickly locked the door and sat on the edge of the counter with my head in my hands. I was trying not to cry. I stood up and looked at myself in the mirror. Why was I putting myself through this? UGH! I exhaled.
"Pull it together bitch. You woke up in that bed. He gave you some bomb ass head and then his ass won the game. Get out yo' feelings," I had to say to myself.

I wanted to throw some water on my face but was afraid of messing up my makeup. I closed my eyes and took a deep breath.

Knock. Knock.
"Just a minute. Someone is in here," I said in the smallest voice possible.
"It's me. Open the door," B's voice commanded from the other side of the door.
Reluctantly I turned the handle and he pushed the door open.
"You ok?" he asked.
"Yeah, I had to use the bathroom. Are you ok?" I asked starting to wash my hands.
"Yeah, I just thought you had left without saying goodbye."
He handed me a cup and looked at me like he knew I was lying.
"Why would I do that?" I asked trying to play it off.
I didn't want him to know that their PDA pissed me off.
"I don't know, and you're not leaving anyway," he said grabbed my waist and kissed me on the back of my neck. I spun around and he began to suck on my bottom lip.
"Don't start anything you can't finish," I said in between kisses.
"Oh, you know I'm gonna finish it, but not until you cum first!" he said.
"You have a whole party you need to get to," I said and tried to break free from him.
I was mad and I hated that his kisses were able to make me forget all the bullshit I just witnessed.

"Everything that I need is right here in this room," he said. I forcefully pulled away from him. How could he even say something like that when he was just kissing her in front of everyone?
"Babe, don't trip about her. I love you; I'm in love with you. She is not even an issue," he said and pulled me back to him.
"I'm not tripping at all," I lied.
"You are, I know you. I will take care of it. Just promise you will stay and be with me tonight," he pleaded.

I looked him in the eyes trying to figure out if he was lying or not. Whenever he was lying he was not able to look me in my eyes. He stared right back at me, trying to prove that he wasn't lying.

"Ok," I whispered and walked out of the bathroom leaving him there. I went back into the party. There were champagne glasses and shot glasses everywhere. I started to clean up, throwing away garbage.

"Oh, I can do that," his girlfriend replied and picked up a plate that I was about to pick up.

"Oh, I was just trying to help B out," I said and backed away from her.

"That's really sweet of you, but the maid will be here in the morning too so you don't have to do too much," she said snidely.

I laughed and just walked away. I found Tanji and started talking to her. B brought me another cup and stood beside me. I guess he witnessed the interaction and was making sure I was ok.

Tanji and I stood around talking about her latest exploits before she decided to leave for a dick appointment. I walked her to the elevator, and when I walked back into the door Iris motioned for me to come upstairs. I followed behind her into B's room and we closed the door.

"I know you're fucking B," she blurted out.

I almost spit out my drink.

"Um?" I responded.

"I know the both of you all. He watched you the entire night. You can't deny chemistry."

I sat on the couch in front of the bed and she sat next to me.

"He really likes you, I can tell," she said. She had no idea how much her words brought me comfort.

"Really? I like him too, but I know he's a hoe," I replied.

"He's really not. I'm sure you're getting to see Bryant and not just his public persona. He's been my best friend since college so that should speak to his character."

"That does speak volumes with your evil ass," I laughed.

Iris was very selective about her inner circle and that's another reason I really trusted B. Iris was an excellent judge of character.

"Don't worry about Briana's ass either. I don't like that bitch."

"Well damn boss lady tell me how you really feel," I laughed.

"I'm serious, and B never really liked her either. She has just been one long booty call that won't leave," she continued.

"Yeah, but he can tell her to," I responded.

"Remember what happened to the last girl he broke up with," she said as if I could forget about Marisol. She committed suicide after B broke up with her. She even faked a pregnancy. Ironically it was on that trip that I became closer to B. I saw him at his lowest and just wanted to take away all of his pain. That experience really hurt him.

"I never thought about how Marisol's death could still be affecting him," I replied somberly.

"Yeah, B is big and amazing but he's super sensitive. Once he tells you about his background you'll be able to understand him better," she told me.

We sat in silence for a while as I pondered what she told me. I drank some more of whatever was in my cup.

"Give me some," she said and snatched the cup from my hands. We stayed upstairs just talking and joking about some of our escapades from the past few months. Iris was the big sister I never had, but always wanted. Somehow she always knew what to say and how to comfort me. Yet, she was avoiding the elephant in the room. She was not telling me why she left work crying a few days ago, closed the Firm, and wasn't returning any of my phone calls. I was glad she was in somewhat good spirits though and decided to enjoy the moment and not pressure her to tell me. I knew she would tell me when she was ready.

"Damn my cup is empty," I said disappointed.

"So is mine." She echoed my disappointment looking into her cup.

"Thank you big sis. You know I appreciate you," I said and hugged her.

"Girl, don't thank me for anything. We're a team. I'm always going to have your back."

There was a knock on the door and Iris got up to answer it. It was Colin.
"Hey ladies, everyone is looking for you all. We're about to toast," he said motioning for us to come downstairs.
"My two favorite girls!" B exclaimed as we walked down the stairs. He motioned for us to stand on both sides of him and handed us each a champagne flute. We held up our glasses as he gave his toast:

To my truest friends for always being in my corner and keeping me sane. I could not have won an NBA title without you all. Just know some major things are on the horizon, and this was just the first of many to come. I love y'all.

We all drank and began to hug and cheer. For the next hour we drank, laughed, and celebrated. It was great to see B happy and surrounded by love after the trials he went through this season.

"So I'm about ready to kick all of their asses out and put your ass in the air," B whispered in my ear.
"And I'm about ready to throw it back to you," I replied.
He laughed and said, "You're so nasty. I love it."
"Ahem, he said clearing his throat. So I love you all dearly, but I'm drunk and tired. So get the fuck out!" he exclaimed.
"Damn Martin!" his teammate laughed.

Everyone slowly began to leave. I went and stood on the terrace to enjoy the view. It was about to be summertime Chi, and I loved my city. It was June so it was cool with a nice breeze. I leaned over the railing admiring the view of the city. I heard the door open and felt someone behind me.

"Damn, you look good bent over like that. Maybe I should take your ass like this right now," B whispered in my ear.
"Boy, you play too much," I turned to face him.

I wrapped my arms around his neck and kissed him. He kissed me back vigorously and it was as if time had stopped. Our tongues danced and found their rhythm. He rubbed my ass and I rubbed his back. I needed him to manhandle me and give it to me like only he could.

"Ahem," I heard someone clear their throat.
"Oh, so she is the reason I couldn't stay tonight?" Briana asked as she stood in the doorway with her hands on her hips.
I walked towards her. B stood in front of me.
"She's going to be the reason you don't ever come back," B responded rudely, "I told you to leave. Why did you come back?" he asked.
"I can leave so you all can talk about this," I said and began to head to the door. I wasn't about to stay around and listen to this bullshit.
"No Sasha. Stand right here," he replied forcefully.
"I came back because I thought we could work this out. I needed closure, but I guess I found it," she snidely remarked and walked towards us. I didn't know if she was about to try to fight me, slap B, or throw some shit so I braced myself.
"Why Briana? You're a gold digger and you've been fucking Lamari this whole time. My teammate? You thought I wouldn't find out about it. Get your thot ass out of my house," he yelled.

"Hmpfh!" she replied. "You stayed cheating on me B. What did you think I was supposed to do?" she wailed.
"Cheat on you? We were never together. You forced yourself on me during a time when shit was low and I just fell for it. I never cared about you like that," he said, taking a step towards her.
I stepped in between them just to make sure she didn't try anything crazy.
"I never lied to you Briana. Just please leave. I don't want you to ruin my good day with this nonsense."

She stopped in her tracks and looked me up and down. "You know what B. You can have her. I'm leaving," she said and stormed out.

He followed behind her, locked the door, and then came back onto the terrace. I was staring at the skyline again, shocked at what had just happened. He came up behind me and held me again.

"Well ok. Why didn't you tell me about that?" I turned around to face him.

"Cause I didn't want you to beat her ass," he laughed.

"You know I would have beat her fake Barbie looking ass," I laughed, "I still will, just say the word." I said and pounded my fist into my hand.

"Nah, she's ok. I'm glad that you have my back like that though."

"Always B. I will always have your back. You're my favorite person in the world right now."

"You're mine too babe."

"I'm sorry," he said. "I told you that I would handle it, and I did. I didn't think she would show up to my place," he continued to explain.

"You know she is a clout chaser. She was going to be here to try and be on your arm and be in the spotlight," I said annoyed.

"You're right. I should have known that. I guess the high of the win took over me," he responded.

"You won!!! You won the NBA Championship!!! When do you get the ring Mr. MVP?" I asked excitedly.

"In a few months. I still can't believe it," he said and sat down at the table. I guess it was finally hitting him. He has just won a NBA Championship!

"We are the championssssss," I said, singing and dancing in front of him. He laughed and pulled me into his lap.

"I won when I got you," he kissed me.

"That was so much game," I laughed and punched him in the chest.

"It's not game at all. I do feel lucky just to have you," he kissed me on my forehead.

"You better cause I'm the best thing you've ever won," I chuckled.

"I don't know. An NBA Championship might be a bit better than you. Maybe a toss up." He laughed and picked me up.

"I can't say that I blame you for the comparison," I said very seriously.

"Woman, if you don't stop playing with me," he retorted and carried me into the bedroom.

"Ohh, you just want to take advantage of me huh?" I said but got undressed.

"As much as I would love to. I am so damn tired," he sighed and got undressed as well.

"That's ok. Just lay here with me and I will rock my big baby to sleep," I said and motioned for him to lie on my chest.

I rubbed his head and his back until he started to snore. I loved that I was able to be there with him at that moment. He needed peace and deserved all of the good things that were happening to him. I fell asleep thinking about the future I would have with B and how proud of him I was. I wanted to lay here forever with him. I was at peace here in his bed.

Chapter Six: Face the Music

We rode back home in silence. I really hadn't talked to Colin about anything other than me being hungry and needing other essential things for the past few days. B's win made me so happy and I was excited to celebrate him. When you love someone you're able to pull yourself out of the darkest pits of hell because they need you. I loved B with every fiber of my being. He was my best friend, and there was no way I was going to miss his championship NBA game.

So, I mustered up the strength to put on my makeup and try to mask the hurt, pain, and confusion I felt. Colin had been amazing. He didn't push me and allowed me to talk when I wanted to. Our comfortable silence was just what I needed and I'm glad that we were able to be alone together. He allowed me to sulk, cry, scream, and drown myself in wine and ice cream. The whole time he just sat on the end of the bed, or rubbed my back and brought me more wine. I loved how understanding he was. He knew exactly what I needed, was able to anticipate my moods and cravings and still allowed me to wallow. I absolutely adored him.
Now sitting in the car, I knew that I couldn't shut people out anymore, especially not Colin. I put my hand on his thigh and tried to nuzzle up to him.

"Hey you," he whispered and kissed me on my forehead, all while trying to keep his eyes on the road.
"Hey, I know we need to talk. I think I'm ready now," I said softly and started caressing his thigh.
It was a red light on Roosevelt and Michigan. With the Beasts winning a championship game, the city was in an uproar and there were plenty of bars around the downtown area. We didn't anticipate this much traffic though.

"Ok, do you want to start or wait until we get home?" he asked. We lived in the suburbs and it would take us at least thirty minutes to get home.
"No, let's just listen to some music and we can talk over a bottle of wine," I replied.
"You sure we won't need whiskey?" he joked.
 "We might!"

The drive home took longer than usual. Police were everywhere in the city, making sure that people weren't trying to loot or cause any chaos. I must say that I am proud of my city because the news didn't report any crazy occurrences. Colin played Sade all the way home. We sang and danced to the songs. He shared my love for music and singing off key. We pulled into the garage and I sighed heavily.

"You do know you don't have to tell me anything right now Iris. If you're not ready then wait. I know I didn't do anything, Or did I?" he asked hesitantly.
I laughed, "Of course not. Let's go in. It's about time I told this story."

He turned off the alarm and took my hand.
 "Let's go sit by the fireplace," he motioned for me to follow him.
"Wait, can I get comfortable first?" I asked laughing at him.
"Sure, Sure. I'm sorry. Don't know what I was thinking," he replied.
I stood on my tiptoes and kissed him on the forehead. I wanted to build up the courage to tell this story to him or anyone for that matter.
It all lived in my head, and I was afraid of how speaking the words would make them real. I took off my clothes and got in the shower. I needed to get my mind right.
I allowed the hot water to hit my skin and bring me some comfort. I tried to practice mindfulness and feel the water on my chest and smell the aromas of the body wash. Even listening to the sound of the water brought me calmness.

The tears started to roll down and I tried my best to stop them, but they wouldn't. The feelings of angst, despair, and disappointment came rushing out and I let out a soul cry.

Colin opened the shower door startling me. He was fully clothed but came inside anyway. My body went limp and I just laid on him. I couldn't move. He turned off the shower and picked me up. He didn't even grab a towel, just carried my wet body into the bedroom. He laid me on the bed.
"Wait here," he commanded.
I could hear him, but I couldn't respond. He brought a huge blanket and wrapped me up like a burrito. He picked me up again and laid me in front of the fireplace. He had set up pillows and wine for us. I laid there for a second knowing that I needed to get this out. He sat at my feet and just watched me. I had my eyes closed but could feel him staring at me. I took a deep breath and let it out.

"Ok unwrap me Colin," I laughed.
He laughed too.
"I didn't want you to catch a cold," he explained while removing me from the blanket. He was so serious. I couldn't help but keep laughing.
"The sound you made scared the fuck out of me Iris," he continued.
"I know. I don't know where that came from. I just started to cry." I teared up again.
"Iris listen, you need to talk to me. You can't keep holding this in. I want to help you, but I don't know how. I'm scared baby," he said with so much sincerity.
I rubbed his beard and then began to rub my hands up and down his back. He was still fully clothed.
"Take your clothes off," I commanded.
"What?" he asked.
"Yeah, I want to feel your body against mine right now," I said and helped him out of his shirt.
"Is this going to help you talk to me?" he asked. He looked at me like I was crazy.
"Um hmmm," I said. I licked my lips and unbuttoned his pants.

"Iris as much as I want you to do everything that filthy mind is thinking of doing right now, I feel like you're avoiding the situation. Talk to me baby," he said laying me down and grabbing my left foot. He started to rub it and I moaned.
"Now you know I can't concentrate when you do that," I whined.
"You have to cause I have to touch you somewhere so start talking woman." He tickled me. I kicked him and he stopped. We sat in silence for a while. I could hear the cackling of the fire and feel its warmth on skin. I closed my eyes and sighed. It was now or never. I need to just tell him I thought to myself.

"So my father may not be my father," I blurted out.
"What the fuck?" Colin blurted as well.

I started to cry again. He laid down next to me and motioned for me to come to him. I laid on top of him and continued to sob.
He rubbed my back and said, "Just let it out baby. Tell me what happened."

I took a deep breath and told him about the lunch I had with my old Professor. I told him about the affair he had with my mother before I was born and how he suspected I might be his child. He even showed me a letter my mother had written him saying that she was unsure about the paternity but wanted my father to raise me since they were getting married. She said that she would always love him and to let me live my life happily.

The letter devastated me. I knew my mother's handwriting and it was legit, I called my mother screaming at her asking her who my father was. She didn't deny it, just said that it was a complicated situation and that she wanted to talk to me in person.

I hung up on her. My dad began to call me incessantly and I blocked all of their numbers. I wasn't ready to talk to them at all.

How could they keep this secret from me? How could they allow this man to tell me this? He was my favorite professor in college. It all made sense about why my mother was so adamant about me going to Hampton and them moving there to support me along with my cousin Naschelle. I always thought it was my father's idea because I was such a Daddy's girl and he didn't want me to leave him. I was super spoiled and it was a great thing that my family moved to Virginia because I always had clean clothes and a home cooked meal. Now my memories were tainted knowing that my mother wanted to move to be closer to her lover and tricked us all.

My mother and I were just starting to get close. She was a surgeon and worked long hours. My father was also a Professor, so he had time to take me to and from school and care for me when she was at work. Now I'm wondering if those 72-hour shifts were real and if she spent more time with her lover than she did me.

I didn't realize that I was rambling out loud until Colin said, "damn this is so fucked up baby." He held me a little tighter and we just sat in silence. It was kind of therapeutic that I told him. These thoughts had been haunting me for days, swimming around in the abyss of mind. Sleep had been my only escape.
We sat in silence for a while. "Have you spoken to your father?" he asked.
"No! I haven't returned any of his phone calls," I said exacerbated
"Well how do you know that he even knows? Maybe this is all news to him too Iris" he stated.

I hadn't thought about that. I really thought my father knew all of these years and hid it from me, but maybe my mother was so much of a trickster that he didn't even know what was going on.

I paced the room as the thoughts began to ricochet in my mind. Was my dad that naive that he didn't know anything about it or was he a willing participant in the ruse my mom was playing? The fire began to dwindle and Colin threw another log in the fireplace. The noise startled me.

"Come sit down baby," he whispered.
I sat down. He wrapped the blanket around my shoulders and sat in front of me with his legs open. I sat in between them. I wrapped my legs around his waist and he started to kiss my collarbone. I moaned.

"Thank you for sharing what's been going on. I fully understand now why you needed to shut out the world. This was a huge dilemma. Just know that you are my world and I don't ever want you to feel like you have to battle anything alone. If you need to vent, yell, or punch me to get some feelings out then do that. I hated not being able to help you. I felt completely helpless," he said and continued to kiss me on my collarbone and rub my back.

"I know," I whispered moving closer to him so that I was now straddling him. I was still naked. He only had on a pair of basketball shorts. I could feel him getting harder and I started grind on his lap.

"I know you are so used to doing things on your own, but I'm here now. I will slay the dragons with you my love," he said tilted his head back in ecstasy. He could barely talk.
"I know," I whispered licking his neck and grinding a bit slower now.
"Can I show you how much I appreciate you?" I asked and licked my lips.
"I don't know if you can, but you can try," he said teasing me.
"Lay back," I commanded.

He did so without hesitation and removed his shorts. He was standing erect and I really wanted to jump on it, but decided to tease him first. I licked the tip of his dick and made sure to suck and slurp just the head going in circles until I heard him moan. I then began to deep throat him, gagging since he was rather large.

"Oh shit!" he exclaimed.

I continued to do that until it was becoming too much and I was about to vomit. I then began to use both hands going up and down and sucking simultaneously until we both found a rhythm.

He moaned and I sucked and gripped harder.

"Fuuuuck," he said aloud as I could feel him getting closer to orgasm. He gripped the back of my head forcing me to take all of his girth as he orgasmed. I swallowed, wiped my mouth, and laughed. He laid there lifeless. I climbed on top of him and laid in his arms.

"Thank you baby," he was able to mutter.

"Thank you for putting up with my shit these past few days." He rubbed my back and it wasn't long before I heard him snoring. I listened to his heartbeat and took a deep breath. I couldn't believe the direction my life was heading in at the moment. It took a drastic turn from me dealing with other people's issues and now dealing with a paternity conundrum of my own. Colin pulled me closer to him.

"Go to sleep babe. We can deal with everything in the morning," he whispered in my ear.

He was right. I synced our heartbeats and drifted off to sleep.

I heard rattling in the kitchen and smelled coffee and bacon. I lay there contemplating if I wanted to get up because it felt so good lying in Colin's arms. He was still asleep with his leg wrapped around mine. I couldn't get up if I wanted to. Wait! How did I smell food but Colin was still wrapped around me? I tried to break free.

"Colin, Colin, wake up," I shook his leg.

"What's wrong?" he moaned trying to nestle me back into his chest.

"Someone is in the house," I said.

He immediately jumped up, wrapped the blanket around him, and moved quietly through the house. My robe was on the couch so I grabbed it and followed him. We went into the kitchen where we smelled food cooking.

"Hey Daddy's baby," my dad said as he scrambled eggs in the middle of my kitchen.
"Dad, what are you doing here?" I shrieked. I had no idea he was coming. Colin and I just stood in the kitchen very surprised.
"Well, since you didn't answer your phone for a few days I decided to come and check on you sweetie. Hey Colin," he stated.
"Hey, Mr. Sandford. Let me go put some clothes on," Colin responded. I was still standing there in shock.
"Come and sit down baby. I know you're hungry and want some smothered potatoes," my dad said and put a plate in front of me on the counter with all of my favorite breakfast foods. He put another plate out for Colin and fixed us both a cup of coffee.

"Dad," I began about to spill my heart out to him.
"No, sweetie. Eat first and then we'll talk," he said. He came around to kiss my forehead. I felt like that kiss made me forget all of my cares. He was my father no matter what. The one who raised me, taught me everything, and still made me feel safe and loved. I really didn't care if he wasn't my biological father because he was the only dad I knew. Colin came back into the kitchen and sat down at his plate.

"Thanks Mr. Sandford. This looks so good," he said and dug right into the food.

"It tastes even better," my dad chuckled.
I smiled knowing that my dad really liked Colin. He always said that Sebastian was not for me. Scooter (Sebastian's nickname) has been a problem since he was a kid he would say every time I called myself going back to him.

They always say that your parents know your friends better than you do, but of course as children we never listen to them. Scooter was definitely a problem, but now I had Colin. It didn't matter how much money or fame Sebastian/Scooter had. He still needed to deal with his mental health issues.

We ate in silence. Colin finished first and began to clean up the kitchen. My dad finished and then started to help him. They talked about B's game and relived the highlights. "Man I wish I could have been there," my dad said.

"It was such a great game. You would have loved it," Colin replied.
I knew my dad was just trying to make small talk. He was trying to read my mood. I wasn't upset with him. If my mother was in fact cheating on him then he was the ultimate victim. I knew that he was nervous to talk to me. Although we had a great relationship, whenever he had to talk to me about something serious he would always tiptoe around the issue.

"Let me go shower and I will be right back," I said and left them both in the kitchen. I figured this escape would allow my dad time to get his thoughts together, but I also didn't want to cry in front of him. I needed to be strong and ready for whatever version of events he was about to tell me. I stepped into the shower and let the hot water hit my skin just like the night before. I took several deep breaths, trying to slow down my racing heart. I knew that I couldn't allow my mind to run wild and create crazy scenarios. It was time to face the music. I showered quickly and dressed in some sweats. When I walked into the kitchen I walked over to my Dad.

"Hey Dad, let's go sit on the couch and talk," I said and grabbed his arm. He really didn't have a choice. I wrapped my arm into his and laid my head on his arm as we walked into the den. I wanted to reassure him that I wasn't upset with him. We sat across from each other because I wanted to look him in the eyes.
"So I know you have questions sweetie," he began.

"I do, but I just want you to tell me what you know and then I will tell you about my lunch date," I said.

He shifted his body on the couch. He was upset. His arms were folded and he jaw was clenched. My dad was a big man. He was about 6'4 with the build of a football player-wide shoulders and a stocky build. He was 55 years old and still looked good for his age because he worked out everyday. I rarely saw my father angry, and only saw him cry once when my Aunt passed away a few years ago. He always exuded strength and confidence, the man sitting before me was angry and hurt. I knew all of his emotions because I too felt them.

"Baby, I didn't know anything about this until that day," he began. He told me about checking his email and receiving an email from Dr. Robinson explaining the affair and how long it had been going on and how he thought he was my real father. That email prompted his phone call to my office that day and when I mentioned having lunch with him, he immediately hung up and tried to convince him not to tell me. Unfortunately, Dr. Robinson did not respond to his email and still hasn't.

"Did the email go into detail about anything?" I asked.
"No, it just said he and your mom knew each other for a long time and obviously it's been going on for longer than 30 years Iris," he said angrily. He got up and began to pace the room. I watched him. I also paced when I was angry and thinking.
"What did Mom say?" I asked.
"Well when I couldn't reach him or you I called your mother. She was at one of those wellness retreats and didn't have her phone. I drove up there to confront her. She is denying it and saying that he's crazy. She said they dated back in high school, but she didn't see him again until you started at Hampton," he explained.
"That's all she had to say about it?" I asked confused.
"Yup! You know how your mother is. If she doesn't want to talk about something she won't," he sounded defeated.
"That doesn't make any sense though. Why would he make up this elaborate ass lie and try to ruin our lives like this?" I asked now joining him in the pacing.

"I don't know sweetie. I'm pissed because I think your mother is lying to me," he said slamming his fist into his hand.

"So you think this man could be my father?" I asked and stood in front of him. He stopped and hugged me. I started to cry again.

"He's not my father," I sobbed.

"I know he's not my sweet pea. I never questioned that. You're my daughter. I know that with my heart and soul," he whispered and hugged me tighter.

"Ok," I sighed.

We hugged for a while. I was so mad at myself for shutting him out. He needed me throughout this whole thing and I selfishly closed myself off to the world.

"I'm sorry Daddy," I said. I pulled away and looked him in the eyes.

"Why are you sorry?" he asked seriously.

"I wasn't answering your calls or even thinking about what you have been going through these past few days." He didn't say anything just pulled me back into an embrace and held me tightly.

"I'm glad you all are working this out," Colin said. We both turned to look at him. I didn't even know that he was in the room this whole time. I laughed.

"Dang Colin. What a way to ruin a moment," I teased him.

"Is that what I did? I didn't mean to. I was just happy you all are talking again," he pulled me into the couch and putting his arm around me.

"Well, thank you for taking care of our stubborn Libra woman over here," my dad chimed in.

"She is super stubborn and bad at expressing her emotions," Colin added.

"Um, I am right here," I snapped.

"She's not bad at expressing them, she just has to feel every emotion and process it before she can talk about it," my father responded.

"Is that what it is? Every time she shuts down I think I'm in trouble."

Colin leaned into the discussion with my father. They continued to talk about my emotional state and the way in which I handled conflict. I ignored them and went into the kitchen to pour myself a glass of wine.

"Bring the bottle," Colin yelled out. I guess he knew me all too well. I grabbed the bottle of Malbec and three glasses. I figured it would be a long morning of getting to the bottom of things; we might as well have wine.
I poured their glasses and nestled back on the couch with Colin.
"So Dad, what did you mean when you said you think Mom is lying to you?" I asked.
I really needed to get to the bottom of things. He leaned back into the couch and placed his feet on top of the ottoman. He was relaxed, which was a good thing.
"Well sweetie I don't think your mother is being forthcoming about this affair. I think that part is true," he replied and drank his wine.
"So you think Mom has been having an affair?" I asked.
"You're a grown woman, but you're still my daughter and I'm not going to discuss private matters between me and your mother." He definitely put me right back in my place. It was silent for a while as we all drank our wine.
"Daddy?" I asked innocently. Colin rubbed my thigh.
"Yes sweetie?" he answered.
"Where is Mom now?"
"I think she's at home. I've been staying at your Uncle's house. Not sure if she knows that I'm here," he responded.
I wondered why Naschelle hadn't called to tell me that my dad was staying with her Dad. We were each other's informants when it came to family business and well just about anything. We had been thick as thieves since we were babies. She was my unofficial twin since we were born a few days apart and our fathers are twins.

"Hmpfh!" was my response. I walked out of the room to look for my phone. It had been turned off since that day and I was afraid to turn it back on and get bombarded by the notifications.

"Are you looking for this?" Colin asked. He held my phone in his hands.

"I am. How did you know?" I asked and took it from him.

"Iris, I know you babe. Let's go back in there with your father before he thinks we're back here having sex or something," he laughed.

"Eww, why would he think that?" I asked walking past him.

"Remember he must have seen us naked on the rug this morning," Colin whispered in my ear as he walked behind me.

"Oh damn," I whined.

When we got back in the den my dad had fallen asleep. I placed a blanket on him and we went back into the bedroom.

"Are you going to call your mother?" Colin asked.

"I don't know yet. Let me turn on this phone and see what type of messages I have."

As soon as I put my passcode in my phone started blowing up with notifications. It did not stop vibrating for thirty minutes. I guess five days without a phone was a bit extreme. When it finally stopped I had 397 text messages, 789 emails, and 107 missed calls and 53 voicemails. I fell back into the bed and groaned. Colin laughed at me. "Well you could just delete everything and not go through it," he said.

"Now you know I'm not going to do that," I said and rolled my eyes.

I absolutely hated notifications and checked everything all the time just to avoid those red numbers.

First I sent Sasha a text and told her that I would be in the office on Monday and not to schedule anything that day. We would spend that day catching up on things. She didn't respond right away as usual and I didn't expect her to. I'm sure her and B were too busy celebrating his championship win.

Next I checked my text messages. I deleted the random ones that were full of coupons and spa deals. That narrowed it down to 323.

The bulk of the messages were from my parents. I read my father's first. His messages ranged from panicking to upset. He just wanted to talk to me and make sure that I was ok. My mother's messages were different. They were immediately accusatory. She was asking me why I agreed to have lunch with Dr. Hampton. Then there were messages telling me not to believe anything that he said and that he was trying to blackmail her. The recent messages were in all caps telling me to call her and that my dad was divorcing her.

"Colin, did my father mention anything about a divorce?" I asked hoping that I didn't miss something.
"No! Why?" he asked.
"Well in these texts my mother is claiming that my father is divorcing her and she's blaming me for it."
"Let me see," he said and snatched the phone from me. I went into the den to find my father still sleeping. I wanted to wake him so badly, but instead just went into the kitchen to grab the whiskey and some more glasses.

"That's my girl," Colin laughed when he saw what was in my hands.
"Shit, I needed something stronger to deal with all of this," I cried.
"Come here baby," Colin said and held out his arms so I could come and lay in them. I sobbed and whined. How could my mother blame me for all of this? Was she just acting out of anger or was she telling the truth about all of this? Colin held and rocked me while I cried.
"You want me to check the rest of your messages?" he asked.
"That would be helpful, but take a shot with me first," I said.
"Ok, what are we taking a shot to?" he asked confused.

I paused for a second to think.
"Well it could be that you put up with my crazy which in turn makes you even crazier," I said and laughed through my tears.
"I'm crazy about you!" he exclaimed.

We both took a big gulp of the whiskey. We didn't have shot glasses so it wasn't an accurate measure, but I just needed to take the edge off.

"Feel better?" he asked.

"I will once I finish this glass," I said and turned up the glass again.

"Well you're home and not going anywhere, so if you want to get drunk, go right ahead. I'll join you," he said also turning up his glass too.

"This is the type of support I need from my husband," I blurted out.

"You'll get this and so much more my love," he said and kissed my neck.

For the next hour we finished the bottle of whiskey and handed my phone back and forth trying to clear all of the messages. We checked all of the texts and voicemails. I didn't even bother with the emails. Sasha and I could go through those on Monday.

We collapsed onto the bed when the last voicemail was deleted.

"Looks like I missed the party." My dad picked up the bottle of whiskey that was on the floor.

"Well we just checked all of my messages and needed some liquid aid," I laughed knowing that I was a bit tipsy.

"I see," my father said and laughed at me.

"Dad you lied to me," I blurted out.

"What?" he asked and pushed my leg so he could sit next to me in the bed.

"Yeah, Mom said that you all are getting a divorce," I whined.

"Sweetie, your mother is very angry right now. I'm sure she is speaking out of anger and hurt," he said as he rubbed my hand.

"So you're not getting a divorce?" I asked. I'm sure I sounded like a little girl.

"I'm not sure yet sweet pea. Your mother and I have a lot to discuss, but again that's between us. It has nothing to do with you," he responded sternly.

"She's blaming me for the divorce," I said and showed him the text messages. He read them in silence and then walked out of the room. I wanted to follow him but I didn't want to eavesdrop on the call I know he was making to my mother.

Instead I called Naschelle. She answered on the first ring. "Bitch, I'm at the airport getting my bag. I'll see you in thirty minutes," she said and hung up on me. I just laughed. That's exactly what I did to her last year when she didn't answer her phone after breaking up with her fiancé.

"Naschelle is on her way too," I said to Colin.
"I know," he responded.
"How do you know?" I asked.

"Baby, you know everyone has been blowing up my phone because they couldn't get in touch with you. I held them at bay for as long as I could," he said and snuggled up to me.

"Ok. Thank you." I rubbed his hand. Before long we both drifted off to sleep.

Chapter Seven: Skeletons

Iris was sleeping like a baby. I'm sure it was the whiskey that made that possible. She was either sleeping too much or not at all. The past few days she was only able to sleep if she drank or took some sleep meds beforehand. I had snuck behind her back and asked B for her cousin's number. Iris had her phone turned off and I wanted to get to the bottom of why my baby was in so much pain. Naschelle told me everything that her father told her.

All she knew was that Iris parents were getting a divorce because of an old professor who claimed to have been having an affair with her mother. I didn't know anything about the paternity and Iris didn't know anything about the divorce. I wasn't surprised when her father showed up. Naschelle told me that he would be coming and asked me for the alarm code. He had keys, but Iris frequently changed the alarm code. I didn't think he would come in the wee hours of the morning and make us breakfast. However, I knew that he fiercely loved and protected his baby girl and I knew I needed to stand down and let them have their talk.

Iris was such a Daddy's girl and I loved that about her. She was strong, independent, feisty, and a force to be reckoned with, but she also knew how to allow a man to be a man. Some women weren't raised by strong men and didn't know how to stand down and let a man take charge.
Iris was the epitome of a woman because she didn't take any shit from anyone, but could be soft and lady like when she needed to. I watched her sleep and thanked GOD for her. She was truly my dream come true. I held her in my arms and tried to go to sleep with her.

"Colin," I heard her father call out to me. He motioned for me to come into the den. I walked down the hall and into the den. It was my favorite space in the house. The floor to ceiling windows gave a great view of the pond in the backyard. We called it the white room because of the white couches, rugs, and decorations. Iris hired an interior decorator and her house looked like one from the magazines.

Her father, Naschelle, B, and Sasha were sitting down on the couch.
"When did you all get here?" I asked and hugged Naschelle.
"We picked her up from the airport," B said. He came over to shake my hand.
"Ok, Iris is sleeping now. Do you all want me to wake her up?" I asked.
"No. We need to strategize before we tell her everything," her father whispered.
"What's everything? What am I missing?" I asked confused.
"Well her mother is missing. No one has heard from her," Naschelle responded.
 "We just listened to a voicemail from her mother that she left her last night. She was begging her to call her just a few hours ago," I said.
"Let me see those texts," her father scoffed. I showed him the phone. He called the number and her mother answered.
"Patricia, where are you?" he asked. There was silence on his end for a while. He was listening intently. We were all holding our breaths waiting for an explanation for this wild and bizarre disappearance.
"Patricia, stay where you are. I really don't care where you are or what you're doing, but leave Iris out of this," he yelled.
"What's wrong with Mom?" Iris said.
She appeared out of nowhere. We all turned around. I was surprised that she was awake so soon. Her father walked out of the room, still holding the phone.
"Nothing is wrong with your mother babes," Naschelle came and hugged her.
"Why are all of you here? When did you get here?" Iris asked flustered. I could tell that her wheels were spinning and her heart was pounding.

She was anxious and confused. I stood behind her and wrapped my arms around her shoulders.

"Well I was definitely worried about you. I needed to come and see your face and make sure that you were ok," Naschelle said, took her hand, and led her to the couch out of my embrace. I went into the kitchen to get her a bottle of water. I could hear her father in the guest bathroom still on the phone. He wasn't yelling, but speaking very sternly to her mother. I bet this is how arguments always were at their house. Quiet arguments so Iris wouldn't hear. Iris liked her water room temperature so I took a bottle out of the pantry.

"You ok man?" I heard B ask on the other side of the pantry door.
"Yeah, I'm just trying to make sure she's ok you know?" I said also and handed him a bottle of water.
"Iris is tough. Just be there, but don't be intrusive. She will want to figure this out on her own," he said. He sat down at the counter.
"I know. I know she's Superwoman and I have been giving her space. Just being here you know," I said placing my hand on my forehead. I was really lost as to how to help her, how to be supportive without kicking everyone out and whisking her away to some island so she could really escape this nightmare.

"Look, just let this all play out. Let her father handle it really. Just be there to hold her when she needs you," he said before he walked out of the room. I sat there thinking about what he said. She didn't need me to fix her problem. She just needed me to be there for her. That I could do. I went back into the living room and handed her the bottle of water.
"Thanks baby," she whispered in the smallest voice I ever heard from her.

I sat in the chair across the room so I can be in the midst but not be in her way. Naschelle was sitting on the floor at Iris's feet. B and Sasha were sitting on the couch next to her. Iris was catching them up about the meeting with the Professor and her father's pop up visit. They already knew everything, but she didn't know that. I watched her body tense up as she told the story. She didn't want to tell it, but her entire support system came to be with her in her time of need. They loved her and she felt safe. She glanced over at me and smiled. I smiled back.

"Are you all hungry? I can order food," I said trying to make myself useful.
"I'm starving and I really want some Harold's. Is there a good one out here in the 'burbs?" Naschelle asked.
"It is, and they deliver," Iris exclaimed. She was so excited when they opened a Harold's a few miles from her house and they actually tasted like the ones in the city, she told me. I wasn't from Chicago, but I definitely get the fascination with mild sauce. It's really good and you can't ever beat a good fried chicken spot. Sasha began taking orders for everyone.

"What's going on with Mom?" she asked sitting up.
"Iris, your mother is fine. She is taking some time to process this whole thing, but she's fine. She wasn't answering my calls, texts, or emails and she turned off her locations so I didn't know where she was," her father said as he walked into the room and slumped into the chair next to me.
"Ok so is she mad at you? It doesn't make any sense for her to be mad at you Daddy," Iris said.
"Well of course she's mad. She isn't controlling this situation," he replied.
"What exactly is this situation? Does it need to be handled?" Iris asked jumping right into fix it mode. I loved that about her. When there was a problem she was all about solutions. She wasn't one to wallow in despair. She wanted to make everything better and everyone happy.
"No, Iris. It's nothing for you to fix baby. Your mom and I just need to work some things out. It's nothing for you to worry about," he said reassuringly.

Everyone looked at each other.
"Why are you all looking at each other like you know something that I don't?" she asked.
She could read our facial expressions. We were all silent.
"Tell me right now what you all are not telling me," she commanded.
Her father cleared his throat.
"Daddy, tell me. I'm a grown woman. I can handle whatever is going on," she pleaded,
"Your mother and I are getting a divorce," he blurted out.
He had blown her off earlier when she asked. She sighed heavily. There was definitely a feeling of apprehension in the room. No one said anything. We just waited for her to process it.
"Ok, do you need me to find you a lawyer?" she asked.
Her father chuckled.
"No baby. I got this," he laughed.
Her phone rang.
"It's Mom," she answered and walked out of the room.
 Her father was about to get up and follow her.
"Uncle, let her talk to her alone," Naschelle pleaded. She was right. Iris and her mother always had a rocky relationship, but she told me that over the past two years they were becoming close and talking more frequently. I never understood what the issue was between them except that her mother worked all the time and Iris barely saw her.
The doorbell rang. I went to answer it and give the driver a tip.
"Good, the food is here. I'm starving," Sasha said and came to help me with the bags. We carried them into the kitchen and everyone followed.
They took no time finding their orders and sitting down to eat. I was trying to wait for Iris. I didn't want her food to get cold, but I also didn't want to rush the much-needed conversation she was having with her mother.
"Does anyone want something to drink?" I offered.
They all responded with nods. They were too busy eating. I grabbed some glasses and filled them with ice. I sat a bottle of whiskey and one of rum in the center of the table along with some coke.
"Pour your own poison," I said.

They all began passing bottles and talking about which brand of whiskey they preferred, I was listening to them, but also worried about Iris. She hated talking on the phone and a half hour had passed since she went into the bedroom to talk to her mother.

"Eat Colin. She's fine," Naschelle said.

She must have noticed the worry lines on my face. Just as I was about to open my bag we heard the bedroom door open. Iris came into the kitchen in tears. She came and sat next to me and put her head on my shoulder.

"What did she say to you?" her father asked angrily.

"She just explained the situation to me and told me that she's happy that you all are getting a divorce because you haven't been happy for a long time," she cried.

"Really?" her father scoffed. He got up and walked out of the room.

"Eat Iris," B commanded.

"I'm not really hungry?" she said sadly and then walked out of the room.

The four of us just sat there letting the silence build up until it became unbearable. We were all thinking that this was a really tough situation on Iris and her father. Divorce is never easy on a family, even when the child is an adult. Iris was also an only child, so she had to go through this alone. I at least had my sister to talk to when our parents divorced. She knew my pain and helped me deal with it. I felt lost, not knowing what to do to help her. B got up from the table but Naschelle stopped him.

"Just give her a few moments, she will be back," she reassured. He sat back in his chair.

"I hate seeing her like this," he growled.

"I know what you mean man," I agreed.

Her father walked back into the room. He sat down and began to eat. We all watched him, trying to feel his vibe or see any traces of anger on his face. He looked up at us and frowned.

"Don't watch me like that. I'm ok. This too shall pass," he said sounding like he was trying to convince himself of that notion more than us.

"Uncle, you don't have to pretend for us. We love you,"
Naschelle said, got up, and placed her hands on his
shoulders.
"I know Shelly. I know," he said and patted her hands.
Iris walked back into the room. "Ok, I am hungry," she
laughed.
"I knew you wouldn't be able to turn down that four piece with
mild sauce for too long," Naschelle laughed sitting back down
to finish her own food.
Iris sat next to me and I placed my hand on her thigh.
"Thanks babe," she whispered.
I knew her food was getting cold so I took it and warmed it up
in the toaster oven. She warned me about microwaving
Harold's. She would always tell me to just put it in the toaster
oven because microwave chicken was nasty. It didn't taste
any different to me until I actually tried it and she was right. I
really only ate fried chicken when I was in Chicago. Chicago
really had the best food. Way better than Miami.
You could only hear chewing and sipping. I guess we were all
really hungry.
The doorbell rang catching us all off guard.
"Who is that?" Iris asked.
"I'll get it," I said and jumping up to answer the door.
We really didn't need any more surprises. Today had been
eventful enough.
When I opened the door I saw a man that looked identical to
Iris's father.
"You must be Naschelle's father," I said and grabbed his
suitcase from his hands.
"And you must be Colin," he replied and extended his hand
out for a shake.
"I am," I said and shook his hand.
Naschelle had snuck up behind me somehow.
"Daddy, what are you doing here?" she exclaimed going in for
a hug.
"Now sweet pea, you think I was about to let my baby brother
deal with this bullshit on his own. You fucking know me better
than that," he said.
Ok. Iris told me that her dad and uncle cussed like sailors and
she wasn't lying.

"What is your motherfucking ass doing here?" her father asked coming to meet us at the door. I just laughed and shook my head. I took his suitcase in the other guest bedroom. Iris knew what she was doing when she bought a five-bedroom house. With a big family I guess she was used to them being around.

"Now you know your pussy ass needs me here," her Uncle laughed. They embraced and everyone walked into the kitchen.
Iris followed me into the guest bedroom.
"Colin, are you ok?" she asked.
"What? Why are you asking about me?" I was perplexed.
"Well my family drama and them all just showing up. I know this isn't what you signed up for," she rubbed my arm.
I pulled her close.
"Listen. I got you." I kissed her on the forehead and held a bit closer.
"I love you," she said and kissed me on the lips.
"Not as much as I love you," I kissed her back.
"Um lovebirds, we need you in the kitchen," Sasha said. She dramatically cleared her throat.
We followed her into the kitchen to find her father and his twin arguing.
"What's going on here?" Iris screamed at them.
"I'm trying to tell your dumb ass father that it's nothing wrong with that wench Patricia. Sorry Iris," he said sounding sincere.
"I just saw her and that man in the parking lot of the Kroger."
"I just talked to her and she told me she was in New York at a retreat," her father exclaimed.
"What the fuck I got to lie for Roland?" he said angrily.
"I'm not saying you're lying Ronald," he said emphasizing his name.
"Then what the fuck are you saying? I'm blind then?"
"I'm just saying that she just told that she was in New York."
"Well she's fucking lying cause I just saw her ass. She's been lying to your ass the whole time," her uncle scoffed.
"What's the fuck that's supposed to mean?" her father snapped.

Nothing. I'm just telling you what the hell I saw. Now take it how you want to asshole," he laughed.

We all started laughing. That was quite a show. It was funny watching them argue and then act as if nothing happened.

"Come on, let's smoke this cigar," her father said and pushed her uncle toward the patio.

"Well that was entertaining," Sasha said.

"Girl this is nothing," Naschelle said sitting back down.

"Wait, where is Iris?" B asked.

No one noticed her slip out of the room. I knew where she was. She was calling her mother.

"Tell me where you are mom," she said sternly into the phone.

She was pacing the floor of the master bedroom. There were pillows strewn on the floor from her throwing them. I just stood in the doorway. I didn't want to get in her way.

"So why did you lie to Dad and tell him that you were in New York? Why are you lying?" she cried.

"What else have you been lying about? Is that man my father?" she screamed.

She slumped on the floor and began to wail. I sat next to her. B, Sasha, and Naschelle were now standing in the doorway. They had to open the double doors to the bedroom.

"What do you mean you don't know?" Iris screamed. She took my hand and held it.

"Mom, you need to tell me the truth and stop fucking lying to everyone," she cried.

By this time her father and uncle had walked into the room. Her father snatched the phone from her and hung it up.

"Dad, why did you do that?" she stood up and punched him in the chest.

He just held her. Her tears stained his shirt.

"Ok, lets just give them some space," her uncle commanded and we all left the room.

Once we were in the kitchen and out of earshot he asked, "what the fuck just happened?"

Naschelle started to cry. He held her and rocked her.

"Sweet pea, it's ok. I know you feel for your cousin."

"This is fucked up," B said.

I was just silent. Was her mother admitting to everything this man had told Iris? Was he her biological father? Her father would be crushed if it were true. I was crushed when I found out about Colin Jr. and he isn't even a year yet. I couldn't imagine not knowing if your thirty year old daughter was yours.

"Her mother has been scandalous since day one. We told him not to marry her ass," her uncle complained.
"Dad, stop it!" Naschelle said trying to calm her father down.
"Hmpfh," he huffed and began to pace the room.
 I poured me another drink. This has been a motherfucking day, and it was only 6PM.
"I think we all need another drink," Naschelle said and lined up shot glasses.
"That's an understatement," Sasha chimed in picking up a glass.
"Should we toast or something?" B asked.
"Well we could toast to your championship win since that's the only thing worth celebrating at the moment," Sasha replied.
"Well don't take that shot without us," Iris said and picked up a glass and handed it to her father.
"Are you ok?" I whispered to her.
"No, I'm not but I'm not about dwell on this dumb shit," she said.
"Wait! We didn't make the toast yet," Sasha laughed.
"Well I can take another one," Iris said and poured herself another shot.
"You deserve it," her father said as he downed a shot and poured himself another one as w
"Ok so let's toast to my bestie and his monumental win. May this be the first of many for the Chicago Beasts," Iris toasted.
"Don't forget he was MVP too," Sasha chimed in.
We clinked our glasses and took the shot. We were drinking Buffalo Trace, a bourbon whiskey, since we drank all of the Jack Daniels at lunch.
"Iris, babycakes, are you really ok?" her uncle asked.
"No, I really don't know what's going on and it seems like all of the skeletons are falling out of the closet," she said.

"Patricia has been lying this whole time. She's been with this man off and on for the past 35 years," her father reported. "Duh motherfucker. I've been telling your dumb ass this forever," her uncle retorted.

"Dad, that's not helping," Naschelle said and shot him a dirty look.
"No! Fuck that. This wench has been ruining his life since day one. Used all of his money to go to medical school and left his ass in debt. I'm glad we put that lottery ticket in my name instead of yours," her uncle said spilling more
secrets. Everyone immediately stopped and looked at him. He was spilling all of the secrets.

"What lottery ticket?" Iris and Naschelle said simultaneously.
"You talk too fucking much when you're drunk," her father laughed.
"Explain Dad," Iris whined.
"On the day you were born, I bought a lottery ticket and won $10 million dollars. I didn't tell anyone but this loud mouth ass over here. He claimed the ticket and we hid the money from your mothers," her father explained.
"How were you all able to hide that much money?" Iris asked.
"We had good paying jobs. No one questioned us," her father replied.
"Oh, so that's where all the money came from?" Naschelle asked.
"Well damn, what other secrets do you all have? I'm not sure I can take anymore secrets today!" Iris exclaimed.
"Listen, all you need to know is that I am your father. I know that for sure," he father told her.
"For real Daddy?" she asked and hugged him.
"For real," he said. That gave us all some relief.
"Sweetie. The only thing that matters is that you were loved and cared for. What happened between your mother and I has no effect on you whatsoever," her father said and comforted her.
"I just want to make sure you're my father. Can we do a DNA test?" she asked.
"You don't trust me?" her father asked shocked.

"Of course I do. I just want to put myself at ease," she explained.
"Ok whatever you want. We can do it whenever you're ready," her father said and kissed her on her forehead.
"Ok Sasha, can you set it up for us?" she asked.
"Of course Boss Lady," she replied.
"Ok so now that all of the drama is over can we finish this damn cigar?" her uncle asked.
"Yes motherfucker!" her father exclaimed. They walked to the patio laughing and joking.
"Whew! This has been too much," Naschelle said and poured another drink.
"Pour me another one," Iris said.
"I think we're about to run out of liquor," I said and went over to check the bar.
"Nonsense, go into the garage. There is plenty of liquor on the shelf," she said pointing to the garage.
"My little lush," I said laughing at the idea of her stockpiling liquor.

I went into the garage and found at least 15 bottles of whiskey. I brought back three bottles since they were all lushes. I'm sure they would go through all three bottles.
"YAY" They all cheered when I returned with the whiskey. I just laughed.
"So B, isn't the parade tomorrow?" Iris asked. She fixed us both a drink.
"It is. It's downtown in Grant Park. I know you all will be there," he said excitedly.

"I wouldn't miss it for the world," Naschelle chimed in.
They talked about plans for the parade tomorrow, played spades, had a dance party, and joked around till midnight. My baby was smiling. That made me happy. She fell asleep on the couch. I had to carry her into the bedroom and undress her.
"I love you so much," she whispered and I pulled the covers over her head.
"Not more than I love you," I replied and kissed her on her forehead.

She was sleeping peacefully and although I was buzzed I couldn't sleep. I took out my laptop to check emails. I had an email from Carmen. What does she want I thought as I clicked on it? I read it and slammed the computer closed. She's here in Chicago and wanted to talk. How the fuck did she know I was here? What did she want? She had access to the account that I used to pay all of the bills. She couldn't need money. She had the house, the cars, and the boat. I left all of that to be with Iris. Iris. I watched her sleep. She was going through so much right now. I couldn't tell her that Carmen was here. She would definitely flip out. I found my phone and sent Carmen a text. She had called and sent several text messages. I wasn't thinking about my phone. I was thinking about Iris.
I sent a return text.

Me: Got your message. I can meet you sometime tomorrow. I'll give details later.
Carmen: Can we have lunch at Park Grille? I can be there at noon.
Me: I'll let you know
Carmen: Ok. I love you Colin.

I didn't bother to respond. I wrapped my arms around Iris and went to sleep.

Chapter Eight: Confrontations

I woke up to the smells of onions and bacon. My daddy was cooking me breakfast again. I rolled over to kiss Colin, but he wasn't there. I pulled the cover over my head and let out a sigh.

My life had been crazy these past few days. All I wanted to do was run away with Colin. Maybe we could go for a few days on his boat.

"Hey sleepyhead. Are we hiding from people again today?" I heard Colin ask.

I peeked my head from under the cover and he was standing next to the bed wearing a towel. Well damn, I thought.

"No, but you can come get back in bed to protect me," I replied coyly.

"If I get back in that bed we're not getting out for a while," he said and kissed my collarbone.

"I am ok with that." I pulled the covers back and revealed my naked body.

There was a knock at the door. "Breakfast is ready!" My father called from the other side of the door.

"Whelp, the captain has commanded us to come and eat," Colin laughed.

"Ok, let me shower quickly and I will join you all," I said and rushed into the bathroom. I showered, brushed my teeth, and dressed quickly. I wanted to eat the food while it was still hot.

Surprisingly, it wasn't my father who cooked it was my uncle. He made fried catfish, scrambled eggs, rice, and toast. We ate in silence, savoring every morsel of our food.

Both my father and uncle were good cooks, even though my mother took credit for teaching my father how to cook. I'm sure they learned how to cook from my grandmother. She was a chef and people paid top dollar for her food back in the day. I looked around at my family and Colin. They were all laughing and getting along. It made me happy. I just hate that it took something so crazy as an affair to get us together like this.

Naschelle and I cleaned up the kitchen, as the men got ready. Today was the championship parade for the Chicago Beasts! The energy in the city was contagious and invigorating. It was a warm June day. The sun was shining; it was 80 degrees, and a clear sky. It was ideal weather for a parade. I had on my jersey with B's number 4 and some shorts. We decided to take the train into the city since we knew traffic would be crazy. B made sure to give us tickets so that we could be in the family section by the stage. We made our way to the Millennium Park Metra station in less than an hour.

Of course the streets were crowded with people. I hated crowds, but had to endure this for my best friend. We pushed our way through the crowds and made it to the back gate where the players and families were waiting. Sasha was already there with B. She waved and motioned for us to stand with them. I felt bad for bypassing the line, but what the hell? Families needed to stay together.

B was quiet. I could tell he was nervous so I hugged him tightly and whispered, "you got this killer."
He laughed and kissed me on my cheek. An usher came and escorted us to our seats. Sasha sat to the left of me and Colin was on my right. With my dad, uncle, and cousin we took up an entire row in the front. B was the MVP so it was only right that his family sit here. His mother would have been there, but his father's cancer was getting worse. I wondered if he had told Sasha about it yet.

The ceremony started at 10 in the morning, and the parade was after. We sat through the ceremony and then got shuttled in golf carts to a reserved space for families at the end of the parade route. It was a surreal experience and my heart swelled with joy. Colin missed the parade because he got a call about an emergency with one of his deals but he promised he would join us for lunch at B's place afterwards.

Colin

It was 11:30 and I was getting antsy. I needed to meet Carmen at noon and the restaurant was a few blocks from the park. I hadn't decided how I was going to break away from Iris and her family. I needed an escape plan that wouldn't cause suspicion. I knew I had to lie and buy myself a few hours. Luckily, Iris was preoccupied with the parade and all of the celebrations and didn't mind the fact that I had to step away.

I told her that one of the deals I was working on was being met with some issues that I had to handle soon. I had already packed my laptop in my backpack so working wouldn't seem too far-fetched. She was sad that I would miss the parade, but told me to go and handle business. I told everyone goodbye and walked the few blocks to the restaurant. I didn't know what the hell Carmen wanted. I just knew I didn't want Iris to know she was here.

I made it to the restaurant in a few minutes since it was so close to the park. I got us a table in the back just in case someone would see us. I sent her a text letting her know that I was there. I thought I had a few minutes before she arrived, but she responded that she was also there at the bar and would be at the table once she paid her tab.
Damn! This was happening sooner than later. I ordered her an apple martini, since that was her drink of choice and me a Manhattan. I needed liquor to get through whatever this was.
"Hey Colly," she said walking up.
"Where's the baby?" I asked looking perplexed.

"He's with my mother," she replied annoyed.
"Ok, so why are we here?" I asked.
"You don't miss me?" she asked answering my question with a question.
"Carmen, cut the bullshit and tell me what you want," I said sternly.
"I want you," she said dropping her head.

There was silence. She stared at me I guess she wanted to see if there was any evidence that I missed her somewhere on my face.

"Carmen, tell me what you want."
"Seriously, I want you."
"What the fuck are you talking about?"
"I think we should give us another try. We are married. We shouldn't just give up on us."
"Are you high or some shit?"
"No! I'm trying to save my marriage."
"You know I only married you because you were pregnant."
"I don't believe that."
"You should. You know it's true."
"So are you saying you never loved me?"

Luckily the waiter came back with our drinks and took our orders. I only wanted some calamari. We had a big breakfast so I wasn't really hungry. She ordered a salad.
"Maybe you should eat more than a salad since you're drinking."
"Aww, you care about me?" she said making something out of nothing.
"Carmen, I don't want you to be drunk and disorderly."
"Just admit that you care."
"Carmen, seriously tell me what you want."
"Again, I want us to work on our marriage."
"Ok, ok let me entertain your shenanigans right now. Who is Colin's father?" I asked.
"My ex," she replied sheepishly.
"The party promoter?"
"Yeah, Kevin."

"You were still fucking him after he beat your ass?
Unbelievable Carmen."
"I know. I know. I guess it was a moment of weakness."
"You're ridiculous to go back and fuck someone who broke
your fucking nose."
She didn't say anything. I felt bad.
"Ok. I shouldn't judge you for that. I apologize."
"It's ok. You're right. Now I've risked our whole marriage."
"Carmen, listen to me. I didn't love you. I know it sounds
harsh, but I didn't. Well I did, I wasn't in love with you though. I
only married you because you were pregnant.'
"I know you loved me Colin. You gave me the wedding of my
dreams and we had an amazing time on our honeymoon. You
don't remember Mexico?" she asked and touched my hand.

Flashbacks of her sucking my dick on the balcony came into
view. I looked at her lips and my dick jumped. It took me by
surprise. Her dick sucking skills wouldn't get her out of this
jam.
"None of that matters when you made me believe I was CJ's
father."
"I honestly didn't know you weren't. "
'So damn did you fuck us both on the same day?"
"I don't remember."
Are you fucking serious? I thought.

I just looked at her. Damn she was really sad about this.
"None of that really matters now does it?" I asked.
"It doesn't."
"Wait, how did you know I was in Chicago?"
"The bank statements. You've been making purchases here."
"Damn, you're looking at the bank statements now?"
"I knew you wouldn't tell me so I had to find out."
"Really Carmen? Ok so what's your plan?"
"I need to convince you to come back home Colin. I know
you're doing a deal out here and it's almost done."
"How do you know that?"
"I called your lawyer."
I chuckled. "He told you that?"

"Yes, but when will you be done?"

"I have no reason to come back to Miami."

"What about your business? The house? Me?"

"Well once we get the divorce underway we can decide on what to do. I think we should sell the house, or you can have it."

"I don't want the house unless you're there with us."

"That's not happening."

"Why are you being so mean to me?" she whined.

I really looked at her like she had three heads. Was she really being serious? She lied about me being the father of her child, had me marry her under false pretenses, and then wanted me to forgive her and move back in? She had to be smoking that shit.

"Carmen. Listen. Let's talk about the divorce. I'm not moving back to Miami."

"I think we should go to counseling."

"That's not going to happen."

"What can I do to make you come back home?"

"Make Colin Jr. be my biological son."

"He's your son. Paternity doesn't matter."

"It matters to me."

"I can't believe this is happening."

"This is all your doing. How do you think I feel?"

"I know this has been hard on you. I just want you to give me a chance."

My phone rang. It was Iris.

"Hold on, I have to take this," I told Carmen.

Me: Hey Baby

Iris: Hey sexy. Where are you?

Me: I'm at this restaurant just working. Where are you?

Iris: We're at Millennium Park. They wanted to take pictures by the Bean.

Me: The Bean? Oh that's nice.

Iris: When we leave here we are going to B's house. Will you be working long?

Me: No baby. Just give me an hour and I will be there.

Iris: Ok. Love you.
Me: Love you more.

Shit. Iris and her family were literally outside. I looked around to make sure that she couldn't see us through the windows. Luckily we weren't sitting by any windows. I picked a good seat. I still shifted in my seat. Fuck! How was I going to get out of here?

"So that's why you're in Chicago? Who is she?" Carmen asked. She was obviously eavesdropping.
"Why are you worried about who I'm with?"
"It's that lawyer chick isn't it?"
"What lawyer chick?"
"Yeah, she lives here. Oh! How could I be so stupid?" she asked herself.
"How are you being stupid?"
"I knew you were fucking her. I knew it last year at your party."
"Ok. I was fucking her last year and when you told me you were pregnant I cut off everything with her."
"No. You're trying to make me feel bad for not knowing you weren't the father and you've been fucking this bitch the whole time."
"Lower your fucking voice."

The waiter came to check on us. We assured him that we were fine and he walked away.
"I left her for you. I was trying to do right by you and look where that got me."
"Does she know I'm here?"
"Yes, she does," I lied.
The last thing I needed was for Carmen to contact Iris. Iris would never let me live it down.
"What's her name?"
"I'm not telling you anything about her."
"Why not?"
"Carmen. Focus. Divorce. What do you want?"
"I don't want to get a divorce?"
"Carmen, The divorce is happening. Get over it."
"We need to work this out."

"Carmen. No! I will give you $150,000. That should be enough for you to find an apartment and get back on your feet."
"That's all that's in the bank account."
"I know. You can have it all."

She was silent. As if she was pondering my offer.
"Will you set up a trust fund for CJ?"
"That's already been done. He will have access to it after he turns 21."

She was silent again.
"Listen, I don't owe you anything. This is being generous. Take it."
"Ok. I will take it, but I don't want the house. I will move in with my mother for now."
"Ok good. I will call Scott in the morning and let him know the new terms."
'New terms?"
"Yes he is already drawing up the divorce papers."
"Damn Colin. Are you sure about this?"
"I'm sure Carmen. Remember you signed a prenup."
"I know," she replied. She sounded defeated.
The waiter brought the bill and I gave him the cash. If Carmen could find me through my bank statements I know my private investigator of a girlfriend would be able to find me if she needed.
"Can I have a hug?" she asked, stood up, and extended her arms.
"Sure."
We hugged and I left out of the restaurant. I needed to get back to Iris and her family. I was glad that this was all over but I had an uneasy feeling walking out. Carmen gave up too easily.

Chapter Nine: Breaking News

"Sasha, get in here," B called from the living room. I was in the kitchen sneaking food. I was hungry and this lunch was taking too long to get started. Everyone was in the living room eating hor d'oeuvres and drinking champagne.
B wanted to have a fancy catered lunch with his closest friends and family to celebrate him being named MVP. I was all for it and helped him plan it. Since Iris shut the office down for a week, I had time to spend with him and help him with all of his endeavors. The endorsements were rolling in and tomorrow he needed to fly to Oregon to the Nike headquarters for his new shoe deal. Between the TV interviews, newspapers, and reporters he was constantly on the go but wanted me by his side. I was happy to be because it made him happy.

I joined everyone for the toast. We were all wearing his jersey. The love and support in the room was astounding. B made his toast and thanked us for the support we had given him over the past year. He gave special thanks to me and Iris for being his backbone and helping him get through some dark times- that made me feel special.

Then I saw her standing in the corner. What the fuck was Briana doing here? B had broken up with her. I was there. I could feel myself getting angry. I had to calm down. Once the applause was over and everyone was done shaking his hand I pulled him close and asked, "Why is Briana here?"
"Her cousin is the caterer. I guess she is helping her out. Don't worry. She's not here with me," he replied and got pulled into another conversation.

I stood there stuck. Did I have the right to be mad about her being there? I mean they have plenty of mutual friends so I'm sure she will come around again. I just decided to steer clear of her but keep her within eyesight. Iris walked up to me.
"Don't worry about her. B adores you," she said hugging me.
"I'm not worried, just a bit annoyed by her breathing my air. You know the old me would have slapped her ass," I replied.
"Oh I know! I'm glad you're just annoyed. B needs you," she stated.
"I know. Let me make sure everything is ready for us to eat," I dismissed myself from the conversation. I didn't want to think about her ass any longer.

The caterer came to announce that everyone could be seated outside on the terrace. It was beautifully decorated with the Chicago Beasts colors and logos. B sat at the head of the table and I sat on his right while Iris and the rest of the family sat on his left. It was a delicious lunch and everyone had a good time. We danced, laughed, and drank until B was ready to kick everyone out. He enjoyed his friends, but he was always ready to kick people out of his house. They joked and called him Martin, but they all left. I helped the crew clean up and said my goodbyes to the family.

"I'll see you at work tomorrow," Iris said and kissed me on the cheek.
"Great! I'm sure we have so much to catch up on," I replied. I was happy to be going back to work. I had been keeping up with emails, but there were so many cases that we needed to handle. I hoped Iris was ready for work to become all consuming.

"Come here you," B said and pulled me into an embrace as we stood in the middle of the kitchen.

"I'm here babe," I stood on my tiptoes and gave him a kiss.
"Damn you're so sexy," he whispered and kissed me back softly.
He pushed me up against the massive fridge. It took up half of the wall. I could probably fit inside of it.

I moaned and allowed him to place my hands above my head.
He held my wrists with one hand and my neck with the other
as he continued to kiss me. He literally took my breath away
and had me gasping for air.
"You want me to stop?" he asked and loosened his grip. I
shook my head no. He continued to kiss and lightly choke me.
He drove me crazy.
"Tell me you love me," he whispered as he kissed my neck.
"I love you, B," I panted.
"Tell me that you'll never leave me," he commanded.
"I'll never leave you," I whined.
"Come here and take those shorts off," he said and pushed
me onto the island.
I took my shorts off as I was told and bent over the island. He
lightly smacked my ass.
"Spread your legs," he commanded. I followed his command. I
felt his fingers in my mouth and sucked on them. He then put
them inside of me.

"Well damn you're already wet," he whispered in my ear.
I braced myself and anticipated his initial thrust. I had to stand
on my tiptoes so he could enter me. I closed my eyes and held
my breath. He entered me and I exhaled. He moaned in my
ear and sent me into orbit.
"Fuck girl," he said as he stroked me slowly.
I tried to match his rhythm but he grabbed my waist and began
to thrust harder and faster. I let out a scream as he continued.
I squeezed my nipples and felt the sensation shoot down to
my clit. I squeezed my vaginal muscles tightly around his dick
and he moaned. The sound of clapping and moans could be
heard throughout the penthouse. I reached down and began
to rub on the hood of my clit. I wanted us to climax
simultaneously and I could feel him getting deeper and going
faster.
"Damn girl," he let out as I threw my ass back into him.
I moaned his name as I felt myself tensing up. I was about to
cum. I let out a scream and he groaned. We stayed in that
position, me bent over the island, until our heartbeats slowed
back down.
"Damn," we said simultaneously and then laughed.

"Ok, let's take a shower and then go to bed. I'm tired," he said.
"Yeah me too," I replied.
We slept peacefully the NBA MVP and his new girlfriend.

The next day I went into the office early so I could make sure Iris had everything she needed. I got her tea from Starbucks and her favorite flowers, calla lilies. I was happy to have my boss lady back in the saddle. I set everything on her desk and awaited her arrival. I decided to scroll through TMZ just to see what was happening the world of celebrities. A headline caught my eye, it read: **Reality TV Star Toni T. murdered outside an LA nightclub.** My jaw dropped.

Iris walked in the office singing. "Good morning beautiful," she said and handed me a Ziploc bag.
"This is from my Dad. He made us breakfast sandwiches," she laughed.
I motioned for her to come around my desk so she could see the computer screen.
"What the hell?" she exclaimed.
We listened to the news story on TMZ and then searched the Internet for more information.
"Get Joseph on the phone," Iris said frantically.
Joseph was her was her contact at CelebBuzz. I frantically called Joseph's cell phone. He didn't answer. I sent him a text telling him to call Iris back ASAP. We sat in silence. I guess we were too stunned and dumbfounded to say anything. Toni T was just in this office a few weeks ago, laughing and being her boisterous self.

"We have to find out what happened. This isn't sitting well with me," Iris said and began to pace the room.
"Yeah, this doesn't seem like a random shooting," I shook my head.

"It's definitely not a random shooting. She was targeted and we have to find out who's behind this," Iris snapped.

Her shooting was all over the news. People were calling it a hate crime due to her transgender status. I wondered if her sudden celebrity status made her a target.

"As liberal as this country claims to be they will still persecute people who want to walk in their truth," Iris cried out.

She and Toni had become friends. They went to lunch, gossiped about people, and had each other's back. Toni always stopped by the office when she was in Chicago. She was recently fired from the show, Bad Divas, for almost fighting another cast member. It was rumored that she was dating a show executive, but there was never any concrete evidence. Iris made sure to squash any of those rumors and to make sure she was not connected to Mr. Lowenstein at all.

"Who could have done this to my friend?" Iris cried out.

I grabbed her elbow and took her into her office. She had to sit on the floor and cry it out. I knew my boss-she needed to process her emotions and then she was going to solve this murder before the police could. I closed the door to give her a moment. I went back to my desk and called B. He was just waking up when I told him to turn to the news.

"Damn, this is fucked up," B said.

I could hear the news playing in the background.

"Yeah, Iris is pretty messed up about it," I replied.

"I can imagine. Toni T was pretty cool," he said.

"Yeah she was," I sighed. B and I had gone to brunch with her and Iris a few times.

I heard the door open and Iris came and sat next to me on the couch in the waiting area.

"Who are you talking to? Is that Joseph?" she asked.

"No it's B," I answered, handing her the phone.

They talked for a moment. I'm pretty sure he was comforting her and telling her that everything was going to be ok.

The motion sensor detected someone outside. I looked at the camera and saw Colin waving. I let him in.

"Baby you ok? I just heard," he said coming and embracing Iris. She handed me back the phone and cried in his arms.

"Wow babe, this has been a crazy week for you," he said rubbing her back.

"I know right," she sobbed.
"So what happened?" he asked pulling Iris onto the couch.
"We don't know. We just know what the news has been saying," I replied sitting across from them in the leather chair. Just then the phone rang. It was Joseph. I put him on speaker. He told us that Toni was shot point blank in the head. Apparently someone walked up to her while she was standing outside of a LA club talking to other people and shot only her. The medical examiners said she died instantly. We asked if there were any leads or suspects and he flat out said no. He rushed us off the phone, which irritated Iris.
"I can't stand his ass," she said.

"Ok so are we going to figure out who shot her or no?" I asked solemnly. This was a murder mystery that I wanted to solve.
"I don't know if I have the mental or emotional capacity to do this," Iris whined.
"Well just think about it. You know that I'll help in any way that I can," I said reassuringly.

We watched the news for the rest of the day waiting to see if there were any recent developments in the story. Colin left once he was sure that Iris was ok. He lingered in the waiting area while we returned phone calls and set up appointments for the remainder of the week. He kept an eye on Iris, and I was surprised at his level of attentiveness. I was glad for Iris though. It was about time someone took care of her, since it was her job to take care of everyone else.

We made it to 3:30 in the afternoon not having any further information on Toni T's murder. Iris made sure to call her contacts all over LA looking for answers.
Everyone agreed that there had to be some sort of foul play, but no one knew why or who was the culprit. I believed she was the victim of a hate crime. Iris combated my theory with exclaiming that it was LA and that they were welcoming of all people, especially sexual orientations.

She was right, but then who would have killed her and for what reason? We wrapped up the day of phone calls and emails. I went into her office and slumped down on her comfy couch. Iris stood up and looked out the window. From our South Loop building we could see a dog park and had a great view of Lake Michigan. I could tell she was trying to decompress from this stressful day, she was going through a lot. I interrupted her silence with a question.
"Boss Lady, do you think Toni was messing with someone she shouldn't have been?"
She thought for a while and then came and joined me on the couch. Crossing her legs she shifted towards me and stretched out her arm.
"That's a really good question," she finally said.

"I mean she was always messing with a married man or someone who was off limits. Maybe someone's wife or husband found out," I continued.
It wasn't far fetched. Toni T was rumored to be seeing a high profile record executive at the moment. One thing I could say about her was that she never messed with anybody that was broke. Sis only dealt with men with endless money. I'm not talking about ball players or rappers; she only messed with owners, like Michael Lowenstein. He was the owner of two major cable networks. She slept her way to the top and benefited from any relationship she had. She had balls, no pun intended.

"You might be onto something," Iris said and jolted from the couch.
She went to her desk and grabbed her phone.
"Let's check all of her social media accounts, especially Twitter. Let's see if anyone left any crazy comments or threats," she said.
"Great idea," I said and went to my desk in the lobby to grab my phone.
It was charging behind my desk at the time.
"Let's look at Facebook first," Iris stated.
We both logged on and began to scour her page for any rude or threatening comments. We immediately found some.

"We need to write these names down," I said and went to write names down on Iris' white board. Half of her office wall was painted with white board paint. She had to write down most things. It was her process, and although it drove me crazy and I teased her about her process, she always got shit done.

We took turns going back and forth to the white board. In total we had the names of 23 people who had left threatening comments on her page within the last three months.
"Ok, we need to do intel on these people and see if these threats are legit," I said.
"I think we need to check her other social media pages and see if any of these people overlap, and if they do then we need to run intel because they've been harassing her," Iris said.
"Right! You're right," I replied.
"Twitter is going to be a beast so let's focus on IG," she ruled.
"We also need to look at fan pages too. She has a few out there now," I mentioned.

It took us over two hours to scour through Instagram with the different fan pages and pages of the show, BadDivas she was on. We had a list of 37 people who left threatening messages on Instagram and began to cross reference the list to our Facebook list. There were 8 names that overlapped.
"Wow, these are some creeps," I stated.

"For real, let's pick this back up tomorrow. My dad and uncle leave in the morning so we're having dinner tonight. Are you and B coming over?" she asked.
"I'm not sure yet. I haven't heard from B since this morning," I said realizing that fact.
I had been so busy that I didn't text or call, and I'm sure he was busy as well, preparing to launch his shoe deal with Nike.
"Well come if you all can. Let me text my driver to come and get me," she sighed.
"Ok, I will text you and let you know what we decide."

She left and I locked up the office. I sent B a text asking him where he was. I knew that he was doing interviews and doing a whole press run. He was waking up earlier than normal and spending a lot of time with his agent since the championship. He hated being a celebrity.
He just wanted to play ball, but it came with the territory. After a few minutes and no response I decided to go home. I had not been to my own apartment in weeks.

I lived in Bronzeville, which was a historic neighborhood not too far from the office. It literally took me 15 minutes on the train to get home. I had a car, but parking was a mess and again it was only a fifteen-minute train ride. I know my roommate was enjoying having the apartment to herself. We were college roommates our freshmen year. She lived in Memphis originally, and wanted to move to Chicago. She was the only woman I could ever live with because she did not have any drama. I took the Metra train and sat by the window. I chose the quiet car where people are supposed to be silent just to decompress from the day. I despised public transportation, but riding in this car gave you the convenience of public transportation without the annoyance of the crazies and solicitors of the Chicago Transit Authority trains. Oh, and the smells of urine and other bodily functions.

When I got to my building I could hear music playing. My roommate loved trap music. I laughed thinking that my retired neighbors loved when we went to work because there was finally some quiet on the floor. We lived on the third floor so the trek was different from catching the elevator to the penthouse.

I was almost out of breath when I reached the top step. When I opened the door, my roommate was bent over the couch, pantyhose down, skirt up, getting banged by the guy I thought was her ex. They were both startled when I walked in the door. I covered my eyes and rushed into my bedroom. I could hear them laughing.
I laughed too. I wasn't mad at her for getting an afternoon quickie.

I wasn't even jealous. B had been banging my back out for the past few weeks and I was hooked.

I showered and imagined B's hands all over me. My fingers traced my clit and I moaned. I was horny and needed a release.

I dried off and stretched out on the bed in my towel. I sighed heavily wishing that it were him next to me instead of this pillow. I rolled onto my stomach and let out a silent scream. My hands slowly found their way to my cave and I traced my lips slowly making my own body tingle. Thoughts of his chest and arms came into my head as my fingers circulated my clit. I could hear his moans in my ear and feel the warmth of his hands on my ass. I began to rock my hips rhythmically and my fingers found their way inside the warmth of my cave.

My entire hand was working now and I thrust my hips into bed thinking of his tongue being there instead. His body on top of mine is the most amazing feeling and his lips on my skin made me quiver. I laid on my stomach and put the pillow in between my legs. I began to grind on the pillow as if it were him. Wishing his hands were on my ass I began to wind my hips. My movements became quicker, more purposeful as I could feel the build up of pleasure.

I let out a small moan and panted, "yes Daddy" as if he could hear me. I used my fingers to mimic the feeling of his dick inside of me.
They moved quickly as I imagined him kissing me and grabbing my ass.
Harder, harder, deeper, deeper, I pinched my nipple and an electric sensation went through my entire body. My breathing became heavy and I knew it was a matter of moments.
"I fucking love you" I could feel him whispering in my ear and I let out the moan of release as my body convulsed. I pulled my hand from between my legs. I licked my fingers and although it felt good my bed was still empty and I wanted him.

I panted, trying to catch my breath. I rolled onto my back and pulled the covers over me. It was barely 7PM, too early to go to bed. I didn't know what to do with myself really. I had spent the past few weeks at B's penthouse whether he was there or not. Sleeping alone was not something that I wanted to do. I reached for my phone on the nightstand. There was no call or text from B. I called him and his phone went to voicemail. I wasn't tripping because he could have been in a meeting and not able to answer. I curled back up into bed and drifted off to sleep.

My alarm clock woke me up. I still used an old alarm clock that sat on the other side of the room. I would never get out of bed if I only relied on the alarm on my cell phone. I would hit snooze 500 times and be late to work. I shut the alarm off and headed into the bathroom. I needed to get ready for the long day ahead of us. This was the season for divorces and hiding infidelities. Everyone wanted to be free during the summer months and who could blame them? Summertime Chi was filled with day parties, block parties, yacht parties, and backyard BBQs. My phone rang and startled me. It was B.
Me: Hey babe.
B: I miss you. Sorry I wasn't able to call you back last night.
Me: It's ok. I figured you were busy with your agent.
B: Nah. Mike had a yacht party last night and I got too drunk and passed out.
Me: Oh ok (I laughed)
B: Come open the door.

He always did this to me. What if I had another man here? I opened the door and there he was standing with coffee and my favorite bagel from the bakery up the street.
"Well aren't you sweet," I exclaimed and took the bag from his hand.
"Not as sweet as you," he said and kissed me on my forehead.
"Ok, don't lay it on too thick," I laughed.
"Hurry up and get ready. I'll drive you to work," he said and smacked me on my butt.

I got dressed while he sat on the bed and told me about the wild night on his teammate's yacht. He described the strippers, the girls running around naked, the liquor, and the famous people who were there as well.

"Why didn't you ask me to go with you?" I asked.

"Well because I didn't know I was going. My plan was to have a freaky night with you but they dragged me there," he said and pulled me onto his lap.

"It's ok. It's not like we have to spend every moment together," I replied.

"We don't have to, but I love being with you more than anyone else," he said and wrapped his arms around me.

I looked in his eyes and got lost. He was my sanctuary.

"I love you too," he whispered.

I sat on his lap and rubbed his back for a while.

"You're going to be late for work," he whispered.

"Damn!" I exclaimed.

When I got to work Iris was already there, staring at the board of names we had created the day before.

"I went through Twitter last night and we have 30 more names to add to the list. 5 overlap, but some of these people were super aggressive towards her," Iris said as soon as I walked in the door.

I didn't even get a chance to put my purse down.

I stood next to her as she recounted some of the Tweets she read.

"I even printed some of them out. These people are psychotic!" she exclaimed.

I read them and was in shock. Her life was constantly being threatened.

People were telling her to die, to kill herself, that they'd catch her in dark allies and that she would burn in hell. I was astonished by the level of hate these people had for someone they had never met. Reading the tweets made me angry. I couldn't imagine someone saying these things to me on the Internet.

"Did she ever mention this to you?" I asked shuffling through the papers.

"She always joked about her haters, but who doesn't?" Iris asked sitting on the floor.

Her plush rug was her haven. This is where I found her after the paternity incident.

"Yeah, the internet isn't nice to most celebrities, but this along with the shooting points in the direction of a deranged person who really hated her transgender status," I stated.

"I need to call the detectives to see if they have any leads," she said jumping up and going to the phone.

I went to my desk to begin the day. Her first client would be arriving in 15 minutes. It was a wife who suspected her husband of cheating, no big deal. They weren't a celebrity couple, just two doctors with a shared practice.

I organized the clipboard of all the necessary paperwork that would be needed for the six clients we would have today.

I made sure to put out water bottles, fruit, and to restock the sugar and cream for the coffee and tea. Although Colin still sent flowers to Iris every Tuesday, we still had a florist deliver fresh flowers weekly. Iris liked for the office to feel homey. She would always say that people are more willing to tell their secrets when they're comfortable. We always made people feel comfortable, and they came, airing out their dirty laundry. I could write a book about the things that were said in that conference room.

Her first few appointments were routine. Women who wanted to find out if their husbands were cheating. One woman had proof, emails and pictures that the side chick had sent.

It was pretty cut and dry too. Iris asked if she needed a divorce lawyer, but she didn't want a divorce. She wanted to catch him in the act to get further proof. I was baffled but we told her we would do some investigating and keep her posted. When she left we just laughed.

"Hey! They keep the lights on," Iris remarked.

She was absolutely right. Infidelity and drama was the business and I liked my salary!

The last appointment of the day threw us for a loop. It was the wife of a well-known alderman in the city. He was up and coming, very good looking, and ran a squeaky clean campaign. I would have voted for him if he were running for my district.

His wife was stoic. Petite and very well put together. She wasn't glamorous, but had a girl next door look to her. She came in with a tear stained face. My heart immediately sank. I offered her coffee and some tissues. She turned them both down and kept her head down when she spoke.
"How can we help you today Mrs. Reynolds?" Iris asked.
"Well, I, I think my husband is having an affair," she said in the smallest voice.

"What makes you think that?" Iris asked and slid the box of tissue toward her.
Tears began to stream down her face.
"I guess you can call it woman's intuition," she cried.

"Ok, what signs has he been giving to make you believe he's cheating?" Iris asked and rubbed her hand.
"It's the late night phone calls, always working late, trips out of town. He claims he's with his campaign manager, but I don't believe him. I think it's just a cover up," she continued to cry.
"Is the campaign manager a man or a woman?" I asked.
"A man," she replied.

"Well just give us all of the pertinent information and we can put a trail on him and do our research," Iris said.
"Ok," she whispered. She began to write down all of the information with a shaky hand. Her phone rang and it was her husband.
"Put it on speaker," Iris mouthed.
Her husband began to tell her that he would be working late tonight at the office and to not wait up for him. She asked him what time he would be home and he responded that he didn't know. She said ok and then hung up.
"Give us the address to his office and we will see what he is doing tonight," Iris said.

It was officially a stake out.

After she left we began to pack up when the phone rang.
Caller: Please hold for Mr. Lowenstein.
Me: Will do.

I motioned for Iris to come by my desk and put the call on speaker.
Lowenstein: Iris. I need to meet with you immediately
Iris: Ok when and where
Lowenstein: I'll be landing in Chicago in two hours. I will meet you at your office.
Iris: What is this about?
Lowenstein: I'd rather not say over the phone.

He hung up. We both looked at each other. We both knew it had something to do with Toni T's murder, but why would he need to meet with Iris?
"So since we will be here for a while, do you want to go and grab something to eat?" I asked Iris.
"You don't have to stay. We will still need to go and check on that alderman after this," she replied.
"Ok, act like we never pulled all nighters before," I snapped.
"You're right! Ok, let's go to our spot down the street," she suggested.

We walked a few blocks to the corner bistro. We both loved their lamb chops As soon as we walked in they gave us our favorite booth by the window and brought us glasses of wine.
"So what do you think about the alderman?" I asked.
"I'm not surprised. He was too squeaky clean. I knew he had some skeletons in his closet," Iris replied as she sipped her wine.
"Yeah, he's too fine to not have a few side chicks too," I joked.
"What prominent man doesn't?" she asked.

I pondered her statement. Did B have a few side chicks too?
"Don't do that," she said.
"Do what?" I asked sheepishly.

"You know who B is and who he has always been," she stated.
"What does that mean?" I asked.
"B has never had one girlfriend since I've known him. Hell you haven't had one man either," she joked. I laughed.
She had a point.
"So you're saying we're both playas huh?" I teased.
"I call a spade a spade," she replied.
"Well damn."
"But B really loves you. He would never hurt you."
"I hope you're right."

Our food came quickly. We didn't have to place an order because they knew it already. We rarely ordered anything different. The lamb chops were so good because they were marinated in a house blend of wines and spices. They melted in your mouth like butter, and tasted even better. It was one of those dishes that you moaned to while eating. We were in food heaven and savoring every morsel. Iris interrupted my foodgasm by saying, "What the fuck is she doing here?"
I turned around to see who the "she" was. I didn't recognize her at all. "Who is that?" I asked in between bites.
Iris took out her phone and looked something up. She showed me a picture of the woman and Colin on their wedding day.
"Oh, that's his wife! " I exclaimed.

"Right! What is she doing here?" Iris said while texting.
I'm sure she was texting Colin and asking the same question. I watched her walk in alone, pretending not to notice Iris. She sat at a table in the middle of the restaurant and kept looking towards the door as if she was waiting on someone.

After about three minutes a stocky middle-aged man in a jumpsuit joined her at the table. He was bald with no facial hair. He gave her a kiss on the cheek and then sat down. I could tell that she mentioned us because he tried to discreetly look our way. I was staring at them though.

I did not want to take my eyes off them. Iris' phone rang and I could only hear her end of the conversation.

She wasn't upset and kept answering, "ok." She described the man that was with her and then smiled. When she hung up the phone I gave her the "Ok what bitch?" look. She laughed.

"She is with his lawyer. She is about to sign the divorce papers," Iris announced.
"Oh. Ok. I thought I was about to have to fight this hoe," I said and picked up my wine glass. Iris laughed.
"No, it still doesn't explain why she is here instead of being in Miami where they both live," Iris said, glancing over at their table.
"This is true, but maybe he had to meet Colin here for some business. Don't trip about it. As long as the hoe signs the papers you have nothing to worry about," I said, eating my mashed potatoes.
"You're right. Let me calm down," she said.
After a few minutes she asked, "you don't think it's odd that they came to my favorite restaurant though? Out of all the restaurants in Chicago?
"How would she know this is your favorite restaurant?" I asked and we both looked at each other.

As if a light bulb went off in both our heads we grabbed our phones and looked through Iris' Instagram page. She tagged herself here on numerous occasions and her page was public. We both looked up.
"This bitch is trolling me," she said.
"She has to be," I said. "Wait, how does she even know who you are?" I asked.
"We were at a party together last year and it was obvious that Colin and I knew each other, but unless he told her about me and where I live she shouldn't know anything about me," she stated.

"Let's go. I need to talk to Colin," she motioned for the waiter to come and bring us the check. We paid and then left. On the walk back to the office she was quiet. I couldn't imagine what was going through her head.

When we arrived at the office there was a car waiting outside. Mr. Lowenstein got out and spoke. The elevator ride to the floor was quiet and tense. I was dying with anticipation wondering what he had to tell Iris in private. We led him to the conference room and waited for him to speak. Whatever he needed to say was painful because he could barely muster the strength or the words.

"Michael, whatever you need to say, please say it. You know I will do whatever I can to help," Iris said breaking the silence.
"I think my wife and daughter had Toni murdered," he blurted out.
We gasped.
"Wait! What?" Iris exclaimed.
"Why would they do that?" I asked.
"How do you know?" Iris asked.
"Our maid overheard them talking about it and told me," he said.
"Is your maid a reliable source?" Iris asked.
"She's been with me for 30 years. I trust her more than I trust my wife and kids," he stated.
"Damn. Why would they have her murdered? You and her were done right?" Iris asked.
"No, we weren't. I was going to buy her a condo in London so that we could be together away from the paparazzi. My wife must have found out," he said and started to tear up.
"Wait, the last time Toni and I spoke she didn't mention you at all," Iris said shocked about the revelation. She was lying. Toni came in to tell her that she thought Lowenstein was cheating on her with another transgender woman named Destiny.

OMG! What if it was Destiny? I sent Iris a text and gave her our signal to check her phone, which was just me fake sneezing.
She replied: I forgot about that.

"Actually Michael, Toni did mention you the last time she was here. Who is Destiny?" she asked.
He looked up knowing that he was caught.
"What does she have to do with anything?" he asked upset.

"Well maybe Destiny found out about Toni and killed her. I mean it's pretty far fetched to think your wife and daughter conspired to kill Toni when they've known about her for a few years now," she stated.

"Destiny doesn't know anything about Toni and yes they would have if I was about to leave my wife for Toni," he argued.

"Wait! You were about to leave your wife?" I interjected.

"Like in divorce her?" Iris asked.

"Yes. I had spoken to my lawyer about it. If I left her she would get nothing. She signed a prenup when we were younger," he stated getting up from his seat.

"Well damn, that is motive," Iris said sitting back in her seat.

We were all silent for a while.

"Have you told the police?" I asked.

"No! Why would I do that?' he barked.

"Well what do you want me to do?" Iris barked back. She never backed down from a fight.

"I want you to investigate and see if there is any truth to this. I want to make sure I'm not next," he sat back down.

He was really stressed out.

"Whoa! Why would you be next?' she asked nervously.

"Why get half or get nothing when you can get it all," he stated. He had a good point.

"Ok, good point. Do you have somewhere to go?" she asked.

"I'm going to go overseas and handle some business there for a few days. Here is the number to my private cell. Call me when you get any information," he said as he wrote his number on the notepad on the table.

"Ok. We will keep in touch," Iris stated and escorted him towards the door.

When he left out of the door we sat in the waiting area.

"Girl what the fuck?" I asked.

"I know right. Today has been too much," Iris shrugged.

"We still have to stake out that alderman too," I reminded her.

"Shit! Let's go now," she said reluctantly.

Iris kept a black Tahoe in the garage for emergencies. She had a driver because she really didn't like driving, but drove when needed.

We headed to the Southside to the alderman's office and parked across the street. He had a store front office so we could see that it was just him and another man sitting at a table with a laptop in front of them.

"He really is working late," Iris said.

"That's what it looks like," I said and took pictures since the passenger side had a better view.

"We should let her know what we see right now," Iris said. As soon as she finished her sentence we watched the other man get up, walk toward the door, lock it, and then close the blinds.

"Maybe they're about to come out?" I shrugged.

"Yeah, maybe he is about to go meet with the woman," Iris suggested.

Then we saw the lights go off. We waited for about ten minutes for them to come out of the office. They didn't come.

"Oh no, you don't think they're in there..," I sighed.

"I really hope not," Iris cringed.

We waited for another hour before they emerged. They embraced in front of the door. They lingered in the hug, more than what men usually do.

"Damn, he's on the down low," I blurted out.

"Fuck! Now I have to tell his wife what we saw," Iris said fist fighting the air.

"Do it in a few days. Don't do it tomorrow," I told her.

"Yeah, this is news I don't want to deliver," she sighed.

We pulled off and head back to the office. Still shocked about the events of the day.

Chapter Ten: Sticky Situations

Today was such a long day. I couldn't wait to get home and talk to Colin about his very nosey soon to be ex wife. I couldn't believe she was trolling me on social media. I decided to drive home to get my mind right instead of calling my driver. It was after 8PM so there wasn't any traffic going home to the burbs. I turned on some Anita Baker and sang my heart out all the way home. My family had returned to Virginia last night, so it would be just Colin and me. My sex drive was off the charts these past few days, and I wanted him to make love to me all night long, but he definitely had some explaining to do. I pulled into the garage and he opened the door. He was waiting with a glass of wine.

"I got your bag," he said, opened my door, and handed me the glass.
"How did you know I was on my way?" I asked.
"Well I called your office and you didn't answer so I assumed you would be on your way home," he stated.
"Why did you call my office instead of my cell?" I asked smelling bullshit.
"I always call your office first if you are at work. You hardly ever answer your cell when you're at your desk," he stated.
He was actually right. Cell reception in my office was horrible so I was never really on my phone.
"Ok," I side-eyed him, took my shoes off at the door, and walked into the kitchen.
"Are you hungry?" he asked.
"Actually no. I had lamb chops today remember?" I asked taking a jab.
"Oh yeah. That was weird," he sounded suspicious and walked into the office to put my bag down.
I walked into the bedroom and began to undress so I could shower.

My bedroom was light purple with a black accent wall. Black is so sexy. I always wanted my bedroom to be sexy and comfortable. My black and purple tufted headboard was the major focal point. I designed it myself. My home was a haven, but my bedroom was my sanctuary.

I headed into the bathroom. I always showered when I got home. It was a way to decompress and after the craziness of the day, I needed to get my mind settled.

Colin was sitting on the chaise when I got out of the shower. I picked up my wine glass from the nightstand and finished it off.
"You want some more?" he asked.
"No, I'm good," I said and looked at him. He had on a t-shirt and basketball shorts. I was wrapped in a towel. I sat on the bed and began to put on lotion.
"You need help with that?" he asked naughtily.
"No, I got it," I responded being spiteful.
He had to answer for both his lawyer and wife being in Chicago without telling me.
"So are you going to tell me what's going on?" I asked.

"Well I'll be honest," he started.
"I hope you wouldn't lie to me," I interrupted.
"I knew she was here. I actually met with her a few days ago," he stated.
I just looked at him bewildered. Was he being serious right now?
"Tell me everything," I snapped.
I sat back on the bed to brace myself for whatever he was about to say. I looked at him. His light brown eyes looked so sad.

He took a deep breath and began to tell me about the lunch he snuck off and had with her during the parade and the terms of the divorce they decided upon.
"Why would you keep that from me?" I asked very upset.
"You were already going through so much. I didn't want to bother you with any more nonsense," he tried explaining.

"It's worse now that you kept it from me," I scoffed.
"Iris, listen. I didn't mean to lie to you. It just wasn't that big of a deal to me. I wanted to handle it and get it over with," he continued.
"Colin, I get that and I wouldn't have objected to you handling your business. You should have just told me what was going on," I stated.
"You're right. I was wrong. I should have told you. Please forgive me," he pleaded and got on his knees.
They sank into the lush carpet and I stroked his head.

"Colin, we can't lie to each other, especially about something so trivial. I do not care about you meeting her for lunch to discuss divorce matters. I'm glad that you all are being civil," I stated.
He hugged me, still on his knees.
"Get up," he said.
He removed my towel and began to kiss my knees and thighs.
"Colin, you can't avoid this conversation with sex," I whined.
"Ok," he replied defeated.

"Iris seriously I thought she was going to come here and turn back around. I didn't know she was staying and I definitely didn't know Scott was here. He didn't even tell me," he explained further.
"How does she know anything about me?" I asked.
"Now that I don't know. I never mentioned you and you never came up in conversation. I'm wondering that myself," he said.
"Does your lawyer know about me?" I asked.
"Yeah, you know Scott is my fraternity brother," he stated.
I vaguely remembered he mentioning that.
"Ok so do you think Scott would tell her about me?" I asked.
"Wait, how did she know you were in Chicago?"
"She claims she found out through the bank statements," he said.
"You all have a joint account?" I gasped.
I was surprised by that admission. Colin didn't seem like the type to give a woman full access to his finances.

"No. She just has access to the account that the household bills come out of. That's the only account she has access to," he told me.
"Oh. Ok," I said still not fully satisfied with that answer.

"So do you think they were just meeting about the divorce? Do you think she signed it? Do you think she will put up a fight? Am I asking too many questions?" I asked.
He laughed. "You don't have to apologize for asking me questions Iris. I can handle your cross examinations counselor."
"This isn't even half of a cross examination. I'm trying to be understanding," I said.
"Well I appreciate you being understanding, and knowing that my intentions were never to upset you," he got back on his knees and opening my legs.
"Well, I'm not going to let you off the hook that easily. You still lied to me about it," I closed my legs.
I wanted to make him work for it.
"It wasn't necessarily a lie, more like an omission. Plus you had too much going on. I didn't want to make this something," he said as he caressed my thighs.
"An omission is a lie," I laughed.
"Iris, you had enough on your plate," he said as he tried to coax me to open my legs.
"You are never putting something on my plate. We have to do this thing as a team," I said keeping my legs closed.
"Ok. Go team," he laughed sarcastically.
"Stop playing, I'm serious," I giggled.
"Ok. I am too. It won't happen again," he said then kissed me.

He was definitely my weakness. His kisses made all of the anger go away.

"Let me show you how sorry I am," he said.
He didn't have to say that twice.
I scooted my ass to the edge of the bed and opened my legs wide. He put them on top of his shoulders and pushed me back into the bed.

The first lick was a tease. He kissed my outer lips and in between my thighs. I could feel his breath on my clit as he hovered there for a minute.
"I love this smell," he whispered.
I moaned. He kissed, licked, sucked, and slurped on me until I came so hard. My legs began to shake and he laughed.
"You ready now?" he asked.
"Ready for what?" I asked confused.

He pushed his dick inside of me, and my body convulsed again. It was something about the way our bodies connected. The chemistry and passion was unbridled. I wrapped my legs around his waist and wrapped my arms around his neck. If he was gonna give it to me, I wanted all of it. There was no escaping. With every thrust he gave me, I thrust back. He was moaning in my ear making me wetter.
I nibbled on his ear lobe and whispered, "Fuck me baby," in his ear. He put it in overdrive and made me cum again.
"Damn, you're so wet," he moaned in my ear.
This man knew exactly how to handle my body. We fucked for hours until he finally came. I was sore and satisfied, in sexual bliss.

I woke up the next morning to Sade playing and the smell of coffee. I showered and got dressed. Sasha and I had some work to do today and I wanted to get the day started.
I had on a white sundress and some strappy sandals. It was still summertime and we planned to go have drinks at a rooftop after work. When I walked in the kitchen Colin was sitting at the table with his laptop working.

"Morning beautiful," he said.
"Morning my love," I replied.

He made me a bagel, some yogurt, and a cup French vanilla cappuccino.
"Aww, thanks for breakfast babe," I smiled and sat down across from him. I turned on the TV.

I was hoping that Toni T's murder was no longer a hot news story and they had moved on to something else. I couldn't take seeing her face and hearing her name again. Then I saw another face that took me by surprise. The D.C. news anchor Sally Robinson was found dead in her car. Strangled. I gasped.

"What's wrong?" Colin asked.

"This can't be happening," I said, picking up the phone to call Sasha.

When she picked up she said she had just saw it on the news as well.

"They got her," I shrieked.

"Who is they? Who is her?" Colin asked frantically.

I told Sasha to meet me at the office in 30 minutes.

"I will call you from the car and explain," I kissed him on the cheek again and rushing out of the house.

I called him on the drive into the city and told him all about my meeting with Sally and the crazy news story she had that she wanted me to fact check and help her bring to the news outlets. I hadn't given her an answer, and I didn't know names or particulars. I knew it was too big of a story to leak and it would not be met without opposition. Those senators and other big names would never let this story hit the media, especially if the sex trafficking was as bad as she portrayed it to be.

"Is there anything that can be linked back to you?" he asked.

"I don't think so. I never told her I would help, only that I would think about it," I explained.

"Ok good. Maybe we need to go away until this blows over," he suggested.

"Let me see how bad it is, and then we will make that decision," I said trying to bring more comfort to myself than him.

I wasn't Olivia Pope. I didn't want to get involved in political scandals, and I didn't have the President of the United States in my bed and in love with me. This was too much.

I parked the truck in the underground garage and noticed a suspicious Crown Victoria parked in the garage as well. I made sure to take out my pepper spray and put my finger on the nozzle just in case someone tried to grab me. I checked my mirrors before exiting the car to make sure no one was hiding on the sides of my car.

"Stop being so paranoid Iris," I said to myself.
When I got to the office there were two detectives waiting to speak to me. Sasha was not there yet. They were standing outside of the door.

"Iris Sandford?" one of them asked.
"Yes, and you are?"
"I'm Detective Connors and this is Detective Smith. We are with the DC Metro police. We need to ask you a few questions."
"Sure come on in," I unlocked the door and motioned for them to follow me into the conference room.

"Would you like some coffee or water?"
"No we're fine," one answered for them both.
"Ok, how can I help you? You came all the way to Chicago to talk to me?" I asked nervously.

"Yes, Sally died a few days ago ma'am. Her murder was a homicide and we are investigating a story that she sent to us a few days before we found her body. We are with the sex crimes division," he said and handed me his card.

"Ok. So I can tell you only what she told me. She revealed that there were some senators and other big names in Washington involved in a sex trafficking and child prostitution ring. She didn't give me names or any further details. She wanted me to help her fact check and bring it to the media. I told her that I would think about it and I never heard from her again," I told them.
"So you don't know anything?" Detective Smith asked.
"No, she never told me names or even how she knew," I answered.

"Did she mention that people were after her or seem paranoid? " he asked.

"She mentioned that she might get killed for the story, but didn't say if people were following or after her," I replied.

"Ok Ms. Sandford, thank you for your time and cooperation. Sorry to barge in on you like this," Detective Connors said. He got up to shake my hand.

"Let me know if you all need anything else," I said and walked them to the door.

Sasha walked in as they were leaving.

"What was that about?" she asked and placed her purse on the windowsill behind her desk.

"They were detectives from D.C. investigating Sally's murder. She's been dead for a few days. Her murder is just now on the news," I said and slumped in the leather chair in the waiting area.

"They came all the way to Chicago to ask you a few questions? That doesn't sound right. They could have called you," Sasha said.

"That's what I said too. I guess since it's a high profile case they didn't want to leave anything to chance," I stated.

"I don't know. Something isn't sitting well with me on this one," she sighed and sat next to me.

"Me either. It's something more to this, but it got her killed so I'm trying to distance myself as much as possible from that story," I stated.

"Ok, so let me run down today's agenda," Sasha stated and continued to tell me about my calendar for the day.

I had to call the wife of the Alderman and tell her what we found out. I was not ready to make that phone call. How could I tell a wife that her husband was on the down low? Now don't get me wrong, I've had a few cases like that, but the wife was always suspecting that her husband may have been gay or told her he was bi-sexual so the news wasn't that shocking.

This man ran a campaign on family values and devout Christianity. This would totally destroy his reputation if it got out. There were a few more phone calls I had to make as well as investigate for Mr. Lowenstein. I think the best approach to that situation would be direct. I would just call and ask his wife if it were true. Sasha thought I was crazy, but why beat around the bush.

"So you're just gonna call and say hey did you kill Toni T?" Sasha laughed.
"That's exactly what I'm going to say," I laughed too.
"Let's see how this works out," Sasha shrugged.
"That we will." I got up and went into my office.
The story of his wife hiring someone to kill Toni T made absolutely no sense. His wife was all about keeping their family together and covering up their scandals. Why would she create one?

I pondered this as I stood in front of the windows in my office. I could see the boats on the Lake. I wanted to be on a boat somewhere in the middle of the ocean at this moment to breathe in the fresh ocean air, listen to the waves, and feel the sun on my face. I loved my job, but some things were hard about it, and this phone call would be a difficult one to make.

"Sasha, can you get the alderman's wife on the phone please?" I asked talking myself into making the call.
She answered on the first ring as if she were expecting my call. I asked her if she'd rather me tell her over the phone or would she prefer to come into the office. She told me to tell her whatever it was right away.

I explained to her how we parked across from his office and saw him and his campaign manager working late. She sighed a sigh of relief, but I told her that wasn't it. I also told her about them turning off the lights and then emerging an hour later.
"Well maybe they turned the lights off in the front and went into the back office to work," she suggested.

"That may very well be true, but we saw them embracing and it was very intimate when they came out of the office," I continued.

"Are you trying to tell me that my husband is gay?" she shrieked.
"Ma'am, I'm just telling you what we saw. We have pictures and videos. I can send them to your email today. Is there anything else you would like for me to do?" I asked annoyed.
"Just send me what you have and then I will call you back,' she snapped and hung up the phone.

"Bitch!" I exclaimed as she hung up on me.
"Oh wow. Who do I have to fight?" Sasha laughed as she stood in the doorway.
"I can't believe she is mad at me for telling her what we saw. She asked for my help, now I'm ruining her life. She ruined her own life when she decided that she wanted to find out the truth about her cheating husband," I snapped.
"People always say that they want the truth, and then when they get it they try to make it out to be a lie," Sasha shook her head.
"My point exactly!" I exclaimed.
"Ok, what's next?" she asked.
"Now I need to call Mrs. Lowenstein and ask about this murder," I laughed.
"Oh, I'm staying for this call. Put it on speaker," she said and laughed too.
I had to go through my email to find her number. When I found it and dialed the number it went straight to voicemail. I left her a message asking her to call me about an urgent matter. If she were indeed a killer, she would not want the call to be recorded. I laughed thinking of the TV shows when people wear wires and get other people to snitch on themselves. She would be crazy to admit to anything over the phone.
"You think she's going to call you back?" Sasha asked.
"We'll see, but let's do some more investigating on who else could have killed Toni T. let's see if there's been anything new on her social media pages," I said.

We took our phones and began our search. There were the same trolls who made comments about sexuality. Some were saying it was God's wrath that caused her murder. Some were convinced that it was a hate crime and there were plenty of condolences. Celebrities were tweeting about her and making public declarations against hate crimes. She would have been happy about the outpouring of love she was receiving. I however wished the love had been shown while she was alive.

"Wait here is something suspicious," Sasha said showing me her phone. It was a tweet from a man claiming to know what happened to Toni T. that night at the club. His tweet read: Man! I was there. I saw the whole thing. It was crazy.

"Send him a DM and ask if he will talk to us," I instructed Sasha. She began to type and the guy quickly responded with a phone number.

"I'm about to put him on speaker," she said.
"Hey, this is Iris. I am a private investigator and friend of Toni T. Thanks for talking to me. I just want to know what happened to my friend that night," I started the conversation. He was hesitant at first, but remembers seeing a white male dressed in all black and wearing a baseball cap walk up to Toni while she was waiting with her friend, shooting her in the head, and then running down the street.
"So you're sure it was a white male?" I asked.
"Yeah it was a white man. I saw his ass," he told me. I laughed.
"Ok, thanks for this information. I will tell the police," I told him.
"Don't have them come looking for me. I don't fuck with 12," he said. I laughed again.
"Of course not. I never divulge information like that," I reassured him.
I hung up. Sasha and I looked at each other.

"Well at least we know the hit man is a white male," she said.

"Yeah, but now I have to tell the police what I know," I said and drummed my fingers on my desk. I called the anonymous tip line and left a message stating that the hit man was a white man and they should look at all of the security cameras surrounding the club. I made sure to *67 when I made the call, hoping that it couldn't be traced.

"Girl, this is becoming too much," Sasha started but was interrupted by the phone ringing. She answered it and handed it to me.

"This is Iris," I spoke.

"Iris this is Mrs. Lowenstein. You left me a message," she responded.

"Yes, I need to talk to you about a rumor I heard. Are you sure this a secure line?" I asked.

"It's secure. What did you hear sweetie?" she asked.

"Well I'm going to get straight to the point. Did you have Toni T. killed?"

She didn't answer right away. Her silence was loud. It was as if she were trying to come up with an answer.

She cleared her throat. "That is a ridiculous question Iris. Why would I do such a thing?" she asked.

"I agree that it's ridiculous. I just have to check all leads that I'm given."

"Well I understand that."

"So are you and your husband getting a divorce?"

"That's even more ridiculous than your first question."

"Ok. Well you know if you need my services then I'm here."

"Thanks Iris. I will be in touch," she hung up the phone.

"She's lying," Sasha blurted out.

"You think so?" I asked.

"Yeah. She's lying, but how can we prove it?" Sasha asked.

"Now that I don't know," I said shaking my head.

There was really nothing left that I could do. Unless there was proof that she hired a hit man, then we would have to let the police do their investigating and pray they found the killer. Until then I wasn't about to drive myself crazy on this wild goose chase.

"Ok, the crazy phone calls have been made. Let's hope the rest of the day goes by fast so we can get to this rooftop party!" I exclaimed.

We went through the rest of our day with clients. There were a few more wives who suspected their husbands of cheating, a husband who needed to send his mistress money and needed it to be hidden, and a daughter wishing to find her real father. Overall, it was a light day.
It was finally 4 o'clock.
"You ready to go to this wine tasting?" Sasha asked from her desk.
"Oh yeah. I've been ready," I said.

We decided to take an Uber to the rooftop downtown. It was on the roof of the Goodman hotel. It had a chic and urban feel to it. We bought tickets for it months ago and it was sold out so B and Colin couldn't join us. It was ok. It was girls' night, well girls' happy hour.

When we arrived there was already a small crowd forming. Unlimited wine for $49 was a great bargain. I was in heaven. The rooftop was divided into two sections, one for the wine tasting, and the other one for regular patrons. We made our way through the dark wines before we saw the crowd moving towards the door. They were frantically awaiting someone to come through the entrance. We strained our necks trying to see which celebrity was at the door. Once the crowd moved, we saw it was B.

"Damn B, I really thought it was Drake or something," I joked.
"Haha," he hugged me and then kissed Sasha.
"How did you get in without a ticket?" Sasha asked. We both just looked at her.
"Girl, he can get into any place he wants. He's the league MVP!" I exclaimed.
He stuck out his chest and made a muscle. He was too much.
"Now let me get a glass so I can get drunk with y'all," he said, going to the bar to get a glass. We weren't drunk yet, but I was feeling the buzz.

"Ok, which wines do you want to try next?" I asked Sasha. "Let's do white wines," she pulled me in that direction. B was right behind us.

We were having a good time, getting wine wasted, and dancing to the music. I needed this night, just some carefree fun with my friends. It was also nice seeing B and Sasha together. I was so glad when they finally got together. All of their teasing and fake disgust over the years was just pinned up sexual attraction. I predicted this way before it even happened.

Before we knew it, it was almost ten o'clock and the wine tasting was breaking down their set up.

"I'm hungry," Sasha announced.

"Me too, and I need some water," I said and walked towards the other side of the bar. They claimed to be at capacity, but created a section for B. The DJ played all of the old school jams. We sang, danced, and continued to drink. Colin sent a text asking when I was coming home. I told him to come and join us instead. I told the waiter his name and instructed him to let him through. It was crowded, but they would let someone with Bryant in. We had our own VIP section away from everyone else.

Colin made it there rather quickly and immediately ordered a round of shots.

"It's Thursday!" I exclaimed.

I had to work in the morning. I did not want to get too tipsy.

"Aren't you the boss?" B teased.

"Yeah I think we should take tomorrow off," Sasha chimed in.

"Hell we might have to if we keep drinking," I said and took another shot with them. I definitely gave in to peer pressure.

"Ok, let's go to the ladies' room," Sasha grabbed my hand. It was time to empty my bladder.

"Order me some fries and some onion rings," I told Colin as I got up.

"Ok baby," he laughed.

Luckily there wasn't a line, but there was only one stall open.

"You go," Sasha insisted.

I was so glad because it seemed that my bladder knew that a toilet was close by. I had started doing the potty dance. She laughed at me while I relieved myself. It seemed like whenever I drank the Nile River came out of me. It seemed like I was in the bathroom forever. When I finally came out Sasha had a crazy look on her face. "What's wrong?" I asked.

"Girl, Colin's wife is here," she whispered and pointed toward the stall she was in.
"Get the fuck outta here," I whispered. We finished drying our hands and hurried back to the booth.

"Colin, your wife is here," I blurted to him.
"What? Where?" he asked.
"Is she following you?" Sasha asked.
"I hope not. I didn't post anything on social media," I said and checked my phone to make sure.
"Let me go find her," Colin stated getting up.

"Colin, I don't think that's a good idea," I said and followed behind him. I didn't want him to confront her in his drunken state. There was no telling what he was about to do or say. We searched the tables and then turned the corner. There were a few private booths on that side. It was dimly lit, nice and cozy. I was trying to look for her in the dark when I heard Colin exclaim, "ain't this about a bitch!"

She was sitting next to someone, but I couldn't tell who because Colin was blocking him from my sight. I came around him and stood at his side. I couldn't believe it either. It was his lawyer.
"You fucking her?" Colin asked and sat down across from them. I was too stunned to move.
"Listen man, I didn't want you to find out like this," Scott stuttered.
"Find out like what? Nigga, you're my frat, my friend and you're fucking her?" he repeated.
"You don't even want me. You want that bitch," Carmen said and pointed at me.

"This ain't what you want," I said before I knew it. I was definitely feeling the whiskey now.

"Baby, she ain't even worth it," Colin said rubbing my back.

"Fuck you and her," Carmen snapped.

Colin laughed. "So Scott when did this start?" he asked. He didn't pay Carmen any attention.

"Awhile ago," he stated.

"So you've been fucking my wife behind my back for a while and handling our divorce? Ok!" he shook his head.

"So that's how she found out about me," I said. It didn't take me long to put two and two together.

"Right! Right!" Colin said. He looked at me and shook his head in agreement.

"Bitch I've known about you since you came to Miami last year," she said and rolled her eyes.

"Listen, I'm not about to be too many more bitches," I pointed my finger in her face.

"You're a bitch and a home wrecker," she snapped.

"Girl, he was with me before you even existed. You were a placeholder," I said and laughed in her face.

"Don't explain anything to her," Colin said and rubbed my thigh under the table.

"Man listen, we don't have to do this here," Scott stated.

"We're not doing shit man. You're fired. Carmen good luck and fuck you. Baby let's go," he motioned for me to get up.

I turned and walked off laughing. We got back to our section and ordered another shot.

"What happened?" B asked.

"Let's just say I lost a lawyer and a friend," Colin said and took another shot.

"Do I have to beat a bitch's ass?" Sasha said.

She tried to get up from the table but B blocked her.

"No girl. That bitch ain't even worth it," I laughed.

"Let's just go," B suggested.

He motioned for the waiter to come over so we could pay the bill. The waiter informed us that the owner said it was free of charge. B gave both the waiter and bartender a $300 tip and we left. Colin and I got into a cab while B got into a car that was waiting for him and Sasha.

Colin was distressed. I couldn't imagine what he was going through. I gave the cab driver the address to my office building. We rode in silence. It was a short ride back to my office.

"I have something for you," I said and dug into my drawer.
"What would that be?" Colin asked.
He sounded so defeated. I pulled out some weed.
"Where did you get this from?" he asked.
"I know a guy. Come on. Let's take a drive," I grabbed his hand.
We got into the truck and I drove to my favorite place on the lakefront. It was where I went to smoke and clear my head. I had never taken anyone there before, but Colin needed this.

I led him to the space out of sight from anyone else. We sat on the rocks, lit the weed in the pipe, smoked, and listened to the waves crashing. For a moment the world seemed to stand still and we were in our own universe. We passed the pipe back and forth until we had smoked the small bag of weed I had. It was still nice out, about 75 degrees. The sky was clear and the view was beautiful.

"I'm sorry I put you through this," Colin said.
He broke the silence.
"Don't be. Again, we're a team." I rested my head on his shoulders.
"We are," he whispered and kissed me on my forehead.
"I'll still beat her ass for you," I giggled.
"And mess up your nails?" he asked and tickled me.
"Oh yeah you're right. I can't do that," I said as I held my hands in front of me admiring my nails.
"Guess I'm going to need a new lawyer," he nudged me.

"I'll call Naschelle in the morning," I replied.
We again just sat in silence, enjoying the view. I didn't want to probe and ask what he was thinking about. I wanted him to be alone in his thoughts. I wanted him to know I would be there by his side when he was ready to deal with this, just like he was for me. I wanted to be his comfort for a change.

"You know what would make me happy right now?" he asked standing in front of me and unzipping his pants.

"Oh really?" I asked licking my lips and getting ready to snatch his soul. He moaned as I licked the tip of his dick and began to pleasure him.
I didn't care that anyone could come down and see us at the moment. It was part of the excitement. More importantly, my man wanted to be pleased and I obliged. It was the least I could do to make him happy at the moment.

Chapter Eleven: Going Back

I had a hangover. I lost track of how many shots we had the night before. The weed didn't help either. There was no way I was going to work today. I turned off the alarm and sent Sasha a text telling her to enjoy the day off. It was nice being my own boss. I pulled the covers back over my head and nestled under Colin's arm. He was sound asleep. When we got back home we showered together and just held each other. We could always be intimate without sex. He made me feel beautiful and safe all the time. After the shower I fell asleep quickly, but when I woke up at 3AM as I usually did, he was still awake staring at the ceiling. The roles were reversed now and I had to play the part of the comforting and supportive partner. He moaned as I pushed my ass against him. I wasn't trying to start anything; I was just trying to get comfortable.

"Don't start something," he moaned and kissed me on my neck.
"I'm not. I just want to get comfortable," I teased.
"Yeah ok," he said putting his hand in between my thighs like he was trying to keep it warm.
"Go back to sleep," I whispered finally getting comfortable.
"Help me," he said pressing his hard dick against my butt. He began to kiss the back of my neck and rub my breasts. I pushed my ass against him and did a slight twerk.
"Open your legs," he commanded.
I did as I was told. He traced my clit with his fingers.
He knew how to tease me and get me wet without even really trying.

With his other hand he pinched my nipples. I turned around to face him. I put my breasts in his face so he could suck and lick my nipples. I threw my head back and moaned. He entered me and I exhaled. He palmed my ass and guided me up and down. We turned over and I was on top. He wrapped his fingers around my neck as I moved up and down on his dick. "DAMN!" he moaned.

I rolled my hips and felt him way inside of me. His fingers were still wrapped around my neck. I lowered my body so that he could also lick my nipples. We caught a rhythm and I was nearing an orgasm.

"Yes, yes," I moaned as his fingers tightened around my neck and he bit my nipple.

I could feel the orgasm building up.

"Don't stop," I whispered as he was fucking me back.

I came and collapsed on top of him. He flipped me over and began to hit it from the back. I arched my back and threw it back catching his strokes. He smacked my ass and came. We both collapsed this time. He rolled onto his back and I found my spot under his arm. Before long we were sleeping again.

My phone kept ringing. I was trying not to answer it, but whoever it was kept calling. I wiggled myself from Colin's grip and found the phone on the nightstand. I had missed calls from Naschelle, B, and my uncle Ronald. I called my uncle back first.

"What's wrong?" I asked nervously.

"Your dad, he's in the hospital," he whispered.

"Who are you whispering to?" I could hear my dad saying in the background.

"Iris, he had a heart attack. When can you get here?" he asked.

"What?" I cried out.

"Just get here when you can darling," he said and hung up the phone.

"What's wrong?" Colin said jumping up.

"They said my dad had a heart attack," I sighed sitting on the bed. I had to call Naschelle. She answered on the first ring.

"Girl, I've been trying to call you all morning. Your dad is in the hospital," she exclaimed.

"I know. I just talked to your dad. What's really going on?"
"From what I can gather it was minor. He went to the emergency room because he was having chest pains and they found out he had a minor heart attack."
"Ok. I heard him fussing in the background," I sighed a sigh of relief.
"Yeah when I was on the phone with my dad they were fussing like normal," she laughed.
"Ok. Guess I'm on my way to Virginia," I said falling back onto the bed.
"Ok baby. Love you twin."
"I love you more, baby," I said blowing a kiss into the phone before we both hung up.
"What's going on?" Colin asked.
"My dad had a minor heart attack. He's ok, but I think I should go and take care of him for a few days," I said begrudgingly.
"I can go with you," Colin stated.
"You sure?" I asked. Being at my parents' house was totally different than being here with them. We would probably have to get a hotel room. I was nervous about sleeping with Colin in my own bed with my dad downstairs.
"Ok, let me call my guy with the private plane and see if we can catch him," Colin said stepping out of the room.

I went into the guest bedroom to grab the luggage and began to pack. I didn't know what to pack or how long as I was going to stay. I was worried about my Dad. I'm sure the stress of this divorce and my mother's cheating was the cause of the heart attack. I should have never let him go home. The argument I was having with myself must have been written all over my face because Colin came and sat behind me. I was sitting on the floor in the middle of my closet. Tears began to fall, and I laid back into him. I had never cried this much in my life.
"Don't you dare blame yourself for this," he hugged me tightly.
"I can't help it," I sniffled.
"We can get a charter jet in two hours, but we have to go to O'Hare instead of Midway so hurry up," he said and kissed me on the back of my neck.

"Ok," I said as I tried to pack.

He jumped in the shower as I frantically looked for pajamas. I always slept naked and couldn't remember where they were. "Iris, go take a shower and get dressed. I will finish packing for you," Colin pushed me toward the shower. My closet was massive and had two doors. One led to the master bath, and the other to the bedroom. I reluctantly showered and got ready. I knew I had to move quickly so we could make the hour drive to the airport.
"Ok, you're all packed. I even grabbed your toiletries bag, chargers, and packed your carry-on," he said as he helped me put on my sandals.
"Grab your phone and sunglasses and let's go," he commanded and headed to put our bags in the car.

I called B on our way to the airport. Of course he was trying to find a way to Virginia to support me as well. I told him to stay and finish his promo tour and that I would call him if I needed him. I told him to let Sasha know that I wouldn't be there for a couple of days and I would call her later.
"She can hear you. You're on speaker phone," he stated.
"Sasha boo. Hold down the fort. I'll call you all as soon as we land," I said.
I told them that I loved them and then hung up the phone.

Colin put his hand on my thigh and drove us to the airstrip where we boarded the private jet. The jet was small. It could hold about ten people, but it was comfortable with TVs, full bar, comfortable chairs that reclined, and all the amenities you could imagine on a private jet. The flight was only an hour long, so it didn't make sense to get too comfortable. I reclined my chair and was about to put my headphones in when Colin waved to get my attention.

"You want a drink?" Colin asked.
"As much as I want one I don't want to show up to the hospital with liquor on my breath," I told him.
"Yeah you're right," he said putting down the beer he was about to open.
"Thank you for doing this baby. I really appreciate you," I said and blew him a kiss.

"We're a team remember?" he said and poked me in the side.
"The best team ever," I replied.
"So if we're a team who's the leader and who's the sidekick?" he asked.
"Well if you have to ask then you're not the leader," I teased.
"Oh, but you know I am and you're the sexiest sidekick," he said coming to my seat and kissing under my neck.
'I'll be your sidekick any day baby," I said bringing his face to mine so I could kiss him. "Now you know I can't resist you," he kissed me back.
"Keep that same energy for the rest of our lives," I whispered.
"Trust I will," he replied and sat across from me.
He grabbed my legs and began to massage my feet. I put my headphones in and closed my eyes. The foot massage was feeling so good. I didn't want it to stop.

Before I knew it, we were in Virginia. Colin grabbed the bags and escorted me to a car that was waiting to take us to the hospital. He shook the pilot's hand and handed him some money. I watched him in awe. He was so amazing and made moves in silence, unlike Sebastian who wanted everything to be a public spectacle.

We got in the back of the car and he held my hand. I guess he could sense my nervousness. I knew my dad was ok because I heard him fussing in the background. He had never been sick before, well not that I could remember-definitely never in the hospital. He was only in his early fifties, too young to be in the hospital.

"He's ok," Colin rubbed my thigh.
I just laid my head on his shoulder until we arrived at the hospital.
"What about our bags?" I asked Colin when we pulled up the entrance.
"He's going to keep them in the car until you're ready to go to your parents' house," he said.
"Ok," I whispered and slowly got out of the car.

He grabbed my arm and led me to the information desk. He spoke to the receptionist and found out my dad's room number. Still holding onto my hand, he led me to the elevator and pressed the button to the eleventh floor.

When we got to my dad's room I could hear him laughing. It made me smile. I opened the door and he was there with my uncle watching a Richard Pryor stand up comedy special.
"Aww there's my favorite girl!" he exclaimed as I walked in.
"My favorite man," I said and kissed him on the cheek.
"Shhhh, Colin can hear you," he whispered and started to laugh.
"Oh, it's no competition. You're the winner," Colin shook his hand.
"As long as you know son," my dad chuckled.
"Daddy, what happened?" I kicked off my shoes and curled into the bed with him. Colin sat in the chair next to my Uncle. They exchanged pleasantries while I doted on my dad.
"I don't know baby. I just had shortness of breath and chest pains all of a sudden. Luckily, this old fool convinced me to come to the emergency room," he said and pointed at my Uncle Ronald.
"Luckily for me your old ass didn't die Roland," my uncle chimed in.
I laughed and laid my head on my dad's chest. I closed my eyes and listened to his heartbeat. He rubbed my back and held onto me.
"Daddy, I was worried," I said in the smallest voice.
"I know baby. I was too, but I'm ok. It was a minor heart attack," he consoled me.
The Doctor walked in the room and introduced himself. He was a cardiologist that studied under my mother's tutelage. He spoke very highly of her and told my dad that he was the best next to her and would take the best care of him.

My uncle scoffed at the mention of my mother. I know why he did it too.
"Where is mom?" I asked my dad.
"She was here when they admitted me. She made sure that they did what they needed to do," he reported.

"Dr. Sandford gave us strict orders to make you our first priority," the Dr. continued.

He told my dad that they wanted to run some more tests to rule out cancer or any other illnesses that he may not know about. He was sending in a nurse to check his vitals again and to take him to get the MRI and other tests done as soon as he left the room.

"Good thing is that your blood pressure is down and there aren't any signs of significant blockages in your arteries. Your cholesterol is up though, but it's manageable," he came over to my dad and checked his chart. I gave my dad the side-eye and he squeezed my hand. I told him to stop eating hogmog and all those other southern foods that no one ate anymore.

"Ok Doc. I'm ready to get out of here," my father remarked.

"We will still need to keep you for another 24 hours as long as your vitals stay stable and there aren't any other concerns. I'll send the nurse in now," he said and walked out of the room. My anxiety was lowered a bit. He was ok.

"Colin, can you please hand me my phone?" I asked. He was sitting next to my book bag. He came and brought me the phone. My dad was put in a wheelchair to go and take his tests.

"Do you want me to come with you/?" I asked.

"No, he's fine. I'll take good care of Pops," the nurse said and rubbed his hand.

She was young and cute. My dad enjoyed her flirting.

"Please do," I laughed at my dad.

He had the biggest grin on his face.

"Tell her you need a sponge bath later," my uncle said.

We all laughed.

"You old pervert," my dad responded as he was being wheeled out of the room.

I called my mother as soon as he was out of earshot. She answered on the first ring.

"Iris baby. How are you?"

"I'm fine mother. Where are you?"

"What do you mean?"

"Why aren't you here at the hospital with Dad?"
"He put me out."
"He didn't put you out. You need to be here with him," I
pleaded.
"He did put me out of his room. He was upset with me."
"Listen well I'm here now and you need to be here too."
"Iris things are complicated between me and your father at the
moment. I am sure he doesn't want to see me."
"I don't care that you all are getting a divorce mom. You used
to run this hospital. Come up here so they can take care of my
Daddy," I whined.

"They know to give him the best care. I already threatened the
entire cardiology team. He is in the best care. I'm keeping
track of everything that is going on and getting hourly updates
on him sweetheart."
"Mom, please come up here," I begged.
"Ok Iris. I will be there soon," she said reluctantly.

"Now why did you go and invite that hussy up here?" my uncle
asked.
"She needs to be here to make sure he is ok," I responded.
"He doesn't want her up here, that's why he put her ass out
yesterday."
"Well I want her here so he has to get over it," I said and
handed my phone back to Colin.
We didn't talk anymore, just watched TV and laughed. After
about twenty minutes my mother arrived.
"Hey my baby," she walked in and gave me a hug. She
smelled so good. She always smelled like vanilla. It was
probably why it was one of my favorite scents. I hugged her
tightly and thanked her for coming. I introduced her to Colin
and they embraced.
"Wow babe, I thought you looked like your father, but you are
your mother's twin," he said as he held onto her.
"She looks exactly like me, acts like me too," my mother
winked.
Her and my uncle pretended as if the other didn't exist. They
always had and over the years I was used to the comfortable
silence they gave each other.

"So Colin, tell me all about you. I remember Iris mentioning you last year when I came to visit her," she winked at me. Colin began to tell her his life story and how much he loved me.

"So you're permanently living in Chicago?" she asked.

"Yes ma'am. I'm looking to move all of my stuff in a few weeks," he replied.

That was news to me. We hadn't talked about that yet.

"So what about marriage? I want some grandkids soon," my mother stated.

"What are you doing here?" my father asked as they wheeled him back in the room.

"Iris called me," she said in the smallest voice.

She picked up his chart and read it.

"Dr. Sandford, it's so nice to see you again," the cute nurse said to my mother.

"Rebecca right?" she asked.

"Yes ma'am."

"Rebecca please tell the head nurse to come in here as well as Dr. Adams. I'd like to speak to you all together so I won't have to repeat myself," she shooed her out of door.

The nurse scurried away to follow orders. That was the mother I was used to seeing. That's why I wanted her here. Shit would get done with her around.

Within minutes a few doctors and nurses were in all my father's room. His room was huge with two couches, a huge flat screen TV, a fridge, microwave, and two bathrooms-one for the patient and one for guests.

"Thank you all for coming so quickly," my mother stood and began to ask them questions. They stood as though she was the general and they were the soldiers taking orders. They explained to her everything they did and why they did it. She began to ask them about tests and results, all medical terms that I was unaware of. Once she was satisfied with the orders she told them to send in the chef so he could take our food orders. They left quickly.

"Do you need anything else honey?" she asked my father.

"No. Thank you for doing that," he said as he adjusted himself in the bed. I got up to help him out. I was in awe of my mother. She was such a boss and even though she had retired, she still ran that hospital.

"Anything you need. It seems as though all of your vitals and tests are normal. No cancer or anything else that may cause any concern. They should release you sometime tomorrow," she said and checked his charts.

"They just ran those tests. How do you know already?" he asked.
"I told them to get the results immediately and to email them to me," she stated.

"Hmpfh," my uncle exclaimed and walked into the restroom. My mom just shook her head.

The chef came in and kissed my mother on the cheek. He told her that once he found out she was coming he was making her favorite jambalaya and garlic Parmesan bread. He told her it would be ready in twenty minutes and he would send up enough for all of us. Just the mention of food made my stomach growl and I noticed that I hadn't eaten all day. 'Make sure to sauté him some spinach and other mixed vegetables. He also needs smoothies made with probiotics with every meal to help with his digestion," she commanded.

"Of course, anything for the other Dr. Sandford," the chef stated and walked out of the room.
"That was impressive Mrs. Sandford," Colin remarked.
"Please call me Patricia or Pat," my mother said coming to my father's side.
"Honey. Are you comfortable?" she asked.
He shook his head.
"Don't think you are bothering them if you need anything. Just push the call button. They are here to make you comfortable," she said and rubbed his head.

You couldn't tell that they were about to get a divorce. She was still his weakness and she did whatever she needed to take care of him. He closed his eyes when she touched him. They still loved each other. I knew that love didn't sustain a marriage, but selfishly I wanted them to work it out. I guess I would have to wait and see how things would play out.

The chef came and personally delivered the food. I would have thought we were in a five star hotel rather than a hospital. He served us on real china with real silverware, not plastic containers like most hospitals. The food was absolutely delicious. I had seconds.
"That was good," my uncle said as he broke the silence that was caused by us all eating.
"It was," my dad chimed in.
"Well I think you need to get some rest now," my mother told my father.
"Yeah, I am kind of tired," he yawned.
"Iris and Colin, are you all coming back to the house?" my mother asked as she grabbed her purse.
"I'm going to stay here with Daddy," I stated.
"No baby. Go home and get some rest. Come and get me out of here in the morning," my dad said.
"I'll stay here with his grouchy ass," my uncle laughed.
"No you take your ass home. I'm tired of looking at your ugly ass," my father laughed.
"Just look in the mirror dumb ass," my uncle said getting up.
We all said our goodbyes. I didn't want to leave my father alone, but it was also getting late and I wanted to shower and lie down.
Colin called the car and told my mother that we would meet her at the house. The driver said that he would be there in fifteen minutes.
"I wonder if they can run my DNA against my dad's?" I asked.
"We sure can. Do you want to follow me to the lab so I can swab your cheek," a nurse said. She overheard my comment.
"Sure," I shrugged to Colin.
"You're Dr. Sandford's daughter right?" she asked.
"I am," I replied.

She led us into a room and sat me down in the chair.
"I need you to sign these consent forms first," she said and handed me a clipboard.
Once I signed them all she swabbed my cheek and put the Q-tip in a test tube.
"Ok, we should have the results for you tomorrow. Just come and see me when we discharge your father," she stated.
"Do you all do DNA tests?" Colin asked suspiciously.
"Actually we do. We have a full diagnostic lab in the basement. Running paternity tests is one of the things they specialize in," she stated.
"Oh ok. It just seemed too easy," he shook his head.
"I assure you that our tests are confidential and accurate," she said trying to ease his mind.
"Ok, well Rebecca I will make sure to find you in the morning.

Here is my card just in case you need to reach me," I said as I reached into my book bag and handed her a business card.
"Thank you will do," she said and walked off.

"Don't you think that was too easy?" Colin asked as he led me to the waiting car.
"What do you mean? " I asked.
"What if your mother could sabotage the results?" he asked.
"Why would she do that?" I asked surprised.
"You saw how everyone in that hospitals answers to her beck and call. They will do whatever she tells them to do," he stated.
"But she doesn't know I wanted to do the DNA test," I replied.
"True. Just get a second opinion if you don't like the results," he said opening the door for me.
'You know I will," I laughed.

The ride from the hospital to my parent's house was only about fifteen minutes. My mother was adamant about finding a house that was close to the university and the hospital. Their ranch was rather big.

It had five bedrooms and six bathrooms. There was a huge backyard with a pool and a Jacuzzi. I was jealous that I didn't grow up here, even though our house in Chicago was nice as well. I asked them why they needed so much room and they responded that they wanted to have room for their grandkids.

Unfortunately I was an only child so that responsibility was all on me. Colin grabbed our bags from the car and opened the door for him. I could smell cookies and hear Anita Baker playing. My mother rarely baked. I was shocked.

"Great you all made it," she said coming and hugging us like she didn't just see us less than an hour ago.
"Where can I put our things?" Colin asked.
"Iris has a room on the far side of the house. I'll show you," she grabbed his hand and led him down the hall.

I went into the kitchen and poured us glasses of wine. One thing I definitely got from my mother was how to keep a stock of wine. She had two wine fridges and a wall full of wine in her home office.

"Iris you read my mind," she stated as I handed her a glass.
"Where is Colin?" I asked.
"He said he wanted to shower and unpack for you all," she said.
"Oh," I remarked and sat at the counter.
"Iris he is fine. You didn't say he was that good looking when we talked about him," she rubbed my back in a comforting manner.

"Yeah he is," I laughed.
Colin had a Cuban father and a white and black mother. That made for a beautiful specimen of a man. He was also muscular and fit. For a forty year old, he took very good care of himself.

"Well when are you two getting married?" she asked.
"Well he has to get a divorce first. Remember I told you about the paternity situation," I said. I had to jog her memory.

"Oh yeah," she looked into space as if she were trying to recall the conversation.

"Speaking of paternity. Are we going to address the elephant in the room?" I asked.

"What do you want to know?" she asked sipping her wine.

"So what happened with you and dad?" I asked.

"I cheated on your father. I will admit. He suspected it, but never said anything. I didn't ask him questions either. I suspected he had his own flings over the years," she told me.

"So who is Dr. Robinson mom?" I really wanted her to explain this to me.

"He's my first love. We went to high school together. He went to Hampton and never moved back to Chicago. I met your father in college, fell in love with him, and then had you.

I always kept in touch with Robinson over the years. We would travel to see each other once in a while, but when you expressed interest in Hampton and your father suggested moving down here I went along with it knowing that he would be here," she said and started to cry.

"Mom, don't cry," I said consoling her.

"I love your father. When I said I was happy about the divorce I was lying. I hate that I hurt him. He has been the most patient and loving man," she sobbed.

"Is Dr. Robinson my father?" I asked trying not to sound crass.

"Iris, I really don't think so, but I did sleep with him the month you were conceived. It's possible, but I doubt it," she continued.

"Ok well we will know soon enough," I sighed.

"Iris I'm so sorry baby. I was going through a thing. Robinson wanted me to come clean and tell you and your father everything. I refused, not wanting to shake your lives up. I didn't know he was on his way to Chicago until your father told me that morning when he spoke with you," she sniffled.

I believed her. My mother was a boss and demanding, but she was extremely sweet. She would never intentionally hurt someone. She was a Cancer, super sensitive.

"Mom, do you love him?" I asked. She hesitated for a moment.
"I do. I'm not going to lie, but I love your father more," she grabbed my hand.
"Wow Mom," I said.
That's all I could muster up to say.
"Iris, I love you so much. You are everything I ever dreamed of. I don't want this to come between the relationship we are starting to rebuild," she said and hugged me.

"Mom, I love you but I'm not going to lie. I am hurt and disappointed. Some secrets need to be taken to the grave," I quoted my grandmother. She smiled.

"You're right and that was my plan, but Robinson wanted to know if you were his daughter. He is the one that put the pieces together and figured it was a possibility. I always thought you were your father's child. You have so much of him in you," she said. I was still in her embrace.

"I know and regardless of this test he will always be my father. No one will know the results otherwise," I hugged her back finally.
"Oh this is sweet," Colin said as he grabbed his glass of wine and joined us.
 We laughed. The oven timer went off and my mother went to take the cookies out of the oven. She baked my favorite, oatmeal raisin cookies.

"Mom you shouldn't have," I said but grabbed one as soon as she took them out of the oven.
"Let them cool off Iris you know better," she swatted my hand. I laughed. I always did this as a child. I ate cookies as soon as they came out of the oven, even if they were falling apart. Colin laughed at our exchange. We ate cookies, talked a bit more to my mom, drank more wine, and then went to bed.

"Are you nervous about the results?" Colin asked when I finally laid down.
"No, no matter what he's my father," I said.
We kissed and he held me until I fell asleep.

The next morning my phone rang and awakened me. I looked at the time. It was 9:37 AM. I guess I needed that sleep. Colin wasn't in the bed but I heard the shower running. I answered the unknown number.

"Baby, come and get me out of here," my father barked.

"Ok Daddy. Let me get dressed and I will come there right away. Have they discharged you?" I asked.

"They said they will discharge me once they talk to your mother. Bring her with you ok? I gotta go they're here to poke me again," he said and hung up the phone.

I didn't like the sound of them not discharging him until they spoke to my mother. I hope it wasn't anything serious. I thought as I stumbled sleepily into the restroom. Colin was in the shower.

"Well good morning," I said as I used the restroom. The toilet faced the shower so I had the optimal view.

"Hey you," he laughed and continued to lather up.

"You should come join me?" he said and opened the glass shower door.

"Not in my parents' house," I laughed.

"I said come shower with me, not fuck me," he laughed with me.

"Ok, but no funny business," I took off my pajamas and joined him under the water.

I washed his back and he washed mine. It wasn't sexual at all, but it was very intimate. I made a mental note to shower with him more often.

"It's about time you woke up sleepy head," my mom kissed me on my cheek.

"We have to go get dad. They won't release him without you," I poured myself a cup of coffee.

"I know. They are giving him an angiogram right now though," she said.

"Why does he need that?" I asked.

"Well his cholesterol levels were concerning. I just wanted to make sure there weren't any blockages in his heart that could have led to the heart attack," she stated.

"Blockages?" I asked very concerned.
"Iris, please don't worry. If I thought it was serious I would be operating on him myself."
"Operating?" I shrieked.
"No, he doesn't need any operation. I was just telling you that if it was serious I would be taking care of him, not leaving it up to another doctor," she said calmly.
"Ok, don't scare me like that!" I exclaimed.

"Ladies, as soon as you're ready the car is outside," Colin announced.
"Ooh, car service. I could have driven us," she said.
"It's not an issue at all. This guy owes me a favor so he's paying off a debt," Colin told us.
This was also news to me. We rode in silence. I was super nervous about these DNA test results, but I didn't want to tell anyone. I was hoping that they came out differently than Colin's.

The smell of antibacterial soap never escaped me. A nurse met us as soon as we walked into the hospital.
'He's getting really antsy and wants to leave," she murmured.
I bet my father was in there giving them hell. He could be extremely stubborn and demanding.
"What took so long? I'm ready to go," he yelled as we filed into his room.
"Roland, calm down. We're here now. You don't want your blood pressure to go up," my mother said and checked out his chart.
"What are the results of the angiogram?" she asked the Dr. who was now in the room.
"There is a small build up due to his cholesterol levels, but with the proper diet and exercise he shouldn't have any other complications," he told her.
"Ok, so what was so urgent for me to come?" she asked annoyed.
"Well we wanted to make you aware that his heart is enlarged," he said putting the X-rays on the board.
My mother studied them closely. She didn't speak for a while and it made me nervous.

"Ok, it could be due to the stress his heart has been under," she stated.
"Oh we agree. We just wanted you to take a look," he said.
"Ok, give us his discharge papers. I will have him follow up with Dr. Anderson tomorrow and get the proper meds. I will take care of him," she said and went to my father's side.
"Ok ma'am. Please reach out if you need anything else," he said.
He was obviously kissing her ass.
"Will do. You did a great job Dr.," she shook his hand.

Nurse Rebecca motioned for me to join her in the hall. I looked at Colin and he followed me. She took me into a private waiting area.

"Here are your results," she said and slid a manila envelope across the table and then walked away.

I handed the envelope to Colin. I was too nervous to read it. He read it and proudly proclaimed that my father was my father. I hugged him and cried. I knew it all along, but my mom had me nervous. I dried my tears and went back into his hospital room.
'Where did you all disappear to?" my dad asked.
I handed him the envelope and he read it.
"Oh baby, I told you," he said as I hugged him. My mother took the papers from him and read them for herself. She began to cry and joined us in the hug.
"This is touching," Colin said. I laughed and went to hug him.
"The car is here," he said to me.
"Ok Daddy, let's break you out of here!" I exclaimed.
There was a stretch limo outside this time. Colin made sure that my parents would be comfortable.
"This is nice Colin," my mother said patting him on the back.
"Thank you baby," I said and kissed him.
"Anything for you," he kissed me back.

We got my father settled in in no time. He just wanted to watch TV in the den in his lazy boy recliner chair. My mother cooked us lunch and we sat and watched TV with my dad for a while.

"Iris, your father is fine. I will stay here and take care of him. You all can go back to Chicago," my mother said. She brought him some water and he thanked her.

"You sure dad?" I asked. They had only been back together for five minutes. I wasn't sure if I should leave them.
"Yes, your mother will take care of me. Go home and enjoy the Chicago weather," he insisted.

I looked at Colin. He grabbed his phone and walked out of the room. I knew he was trying to get us a ride home. I loved how he handled things and I didn't have to worry about booking flights.
"We can leave in the morning," he announced when he walked back in.

"Great. I will cook tonight and we can have a nice family dinner," my mother rejoiced.

I sat and watched TV with my dad. Colin and my mom went into the kitchen to start dinner.
The roles were reversed, as it was usually my dad who did all of the cooking. My dad and I watched a documentary on the Civil Rights movement. That was our thing. We watched documentaries and argued politics. I curled up on the couch and enjoyed the time just being with my parents. Work always had me too busy. It was nice to just chill and watch TV. Being home with my parents soothed my soul.

After an hour or so my mother announced that the food was ready. She brought our plates to us in the den and she and Colin joined us. We watched movies and drank wine. My parents liked Colin and he fit right in.
"Hopefully the next time you all come there will be a bun in the oven," my mother said seriously.
"Mother, if it happens it will happen, but can Colin and I enjoy each other for a while," I asked.
"I actually want to have kids as soon as possible," Colin said. His announcement shocked me.
"Um really?" I asked.

"Yeah baby, I'm 40. I need to start now," he laughed.
"Oh damn," I hadn't thought about his age. I forgot he was ten years older than me sometimes.
"Well that settles it. We need to have some grandchildren running around here," my father joined in.
"Oh so you all are ganging up on me now huh?" I laughed.
"Yes sweetie. You're 30 now. Let's get some babies going," my mother stated.
"If and when I have a baby you are moving to Chicago to help out," I told them.
"Deal," they said simultaneously. I didn't think it would be that easy. I just shook my head at them.

My father began to yawn. My mother helped him to their bedroom. I didn't ask any questions, but they were talking about grandchildren so I took it as a sign that they were going to stay together.
"You want to start practicing tonight?" Colin asked slyly.
"Not in my parents' house," I whined.
"Ok, let's get some sleep. The plane will be ready at 6AM. Can you handle that early of a time?" he teased me.
"Sure can," I said and led him to our room.
Luckily it was on the opposite side of the house, cause we put some practice in that night.

Chapter Twelve: Conclusions

Iris was gone to Virginia with her father and all hell was breaking loose on the Internet. Between the conspiracy theories surrounding Sally's death and people claiming to know who killed Toni T. I couldn't keep up. B was in Oregon at Nike's headquarters again so I was left alone with nothing but time on my hands. I scoured the Internet trying to find leads to either murder. I was hoping that it was just a coincidence that both ladies had come to see Iris the same morning. Were their murders connected? I found myself going down the rabbit hole of Internet searches and ended up finding out more about both women than I cared to know about.

I found Twitter exchanges between Toni and Seth, Lowenstein's son in law that started in 2013. They were flirting with each other. I was shocked and appalled at that discovery. Could that have been motive for the murder? I couldn't wait for Iris to come home so I could share my findings with her. My phone rang, bringing me back to reality. It was B.

"Hey baby, what you doing?" he asked on Face time.
"Missing you like crazy," I responded.
"Man. I can't wait to get home to you."
"When are you coming home?"
"Hopefully tomorrow. I sent you the final shoe designs. Let me know what you think."
I checked my email and squealed. "Babe, these are so dope!"
"You think so?"
"I know so. These are going to be the hottest shoes of the summer."
"Good because they come out in a few weeks."
"Aww shit. My baby has his own shoe."
"Fucking bout time."

"Hey you know everything happens at the right time."
"Speaking of right time. What you wearing?
"Nothing."
"Let me see her."
I laughed, pulled back the cover and put the phone up to my pussy.
"I miss you too baby."
"Really B?" I asked putting the phone back up to my face.
"Put it back and play with it."

I did as he requested. I licked my fingers and put two inside of me, letting him see the juices and hear the noise. I rubbed my clit with my thumb and got lost in the feeling.
"That's enough. I didn't tell you to cum," he barked.
"Ok. Ok."
"Now when you go to sleep you can dream about me."
"I always do."
"Goodnight beautiful."
'Goodnight my love."

I blew him a kiss and hung up the phone. He had only been gone for three days but I missed him so much. He was crazy to think that I wouldn't finish off without him. I grabbed the vibrator from my nightstand and made myself cum thinking about him. I drifted off to sleep with a smile on my face.

I groggily woke up and felt sick to my stomach. I had eaten some Thai food the night before and maybe it wasn't agreeing with me. It all came up. My roommate heard me and held my hair.
"Are you pregnant?" she asked jokingly.
"No, I'm not pregnant," I snapped.
"Ok well let me get you some ginger ale. Go lay back down," she said and left the room.

I tried to brush my teeth but I was right back hugging the toilet. I felt so nauseous and drained. After about a half hour, I was finally able to brush my teeth and shower. It took all of my energy. When I got back to my room she was there holding a pregnancy test.

"Go pee on the stick," she commanded.
"I don't think I have anything else left in me," I cried.
She handed me a bottle of water. I drank it and laid down.
"When you have to pee, don't forget to take this with you," she laughed.
"I'm going to get you some crackers and more ginger ale. I'll be back," she said I heard her grab her keys and walk out of the door.
I knew I wasn't pregnant. I was on birth control. I went to go get my shot faithfully every three months. I looked at the calendar on my phone and realized I was supposed to go last month to get the shot, but I was so preoccupied with the drama of the Firm.
"Fuck!" I screamed kicking off the covers. I had to know if I was pregnant now. My phone rang and it was Iris.
"Hey baby what you doing?" she asked.
"About to take a pregnancy test," I whined.
"What? I'm on my way," she said shrieked and hung up on me.

I forced myself to pee on the stick but it was such a small amount. I paced the room and bit my nails waiting for the time to pass. It took everything in me not to stare at the space on the pregnancy test. The lines were faint and I couldn't tell if it was one or two lines. Was it a plus sign?
I wrestled with the thought of calling B and telling him what was going on. I ultimately decided against it. This was a conversation we needed to have face to face.

My roommate came back just in time to read the test.
"It's positive," she and handed it to me. I snatched it from her. Damn! It was a plus sign too.
"OHMYGOD!" I screamed.
"Girl you're carrying Bryant's baby. Why are you upset?" she asked.
"I'm not ready for a baby. This might be a false positive," I said.
There was a knock on the door. It was Iris. She came with two more tests, some snacks, sparkling grape juice, and champagne.

"What is the champagne for?" I asked.
"I figured we would celebrate either way," she said.
"Ugh" I moaned and handed her the first test.
"Ok I brought two more. Are you hungry?" she asked.
The thought of food made me sick to my stomach. I ran to the bathroom again. The sounds of me hurling echoed throughout the house.
"Yeah she's pregnant," my roommate laughed.
Iris came into the bathroom to check on me.
"When did this start?" she asked and handed me a face towel.
"Just this morning. I was fine yesterday. I even had some tequila," I whined.
"Come on. Let's get you back in bed," she said and helped me to the bed.
"When did you get back?" I asked.
"This morning. I was on my way to work and was going to come and pick you up on the way," she stated.
"I'm sorry," I said.
"Don't you dare apologize. Remember my pregnancy scare?" she laughed.
"I'm glad you weren't pregnant. Could you imagine having a baby by Sebastian?" I laughed.
"GOD was on my side cause whew! I dodged a bullet."
"I think we all did."
"Ok get back in bed. I can go hold down the fort," she said.
"No, I have so much to tell you," I whined.

"Ok. Scoot over," she took off her shoes and climbed in bed with me.
I told her all about the tweets I found that dated back to 2013.
"So you think that Toni T. was messing around with Seth and Michael?" she asked as she read the tweets.
"I don't know, but wasn't this before she began to transition?" I asked.
"No she was already in the process and already messing around with Michael. She should have known that he was his son in law," Iris stated.
"So what do you think this was about?" I asked.

"Toni probably saw this flirting as a means to an end and a way to possibly hold something over the family's head," she said.
"If that's the case it's more motive for Mrs. Lowenstein to have her killed," I wondered aloud.
"Right! If Toni was really messing with Seth it would give Michael motive, no his wife."
"Exactly."
"But Michael was too shaken up. He was in with Toni."
"True, but there is still a missing piece to this puzzle," Iris said.
"Yeah, one plus one isn't equaling two."
We sat in silence for a while thinking what could be the missing link to this story.

"Anyways, how is your dad?" I broke the silence. We didn't talk while she was gone so I needed to know that he was ok.
"Fine. It was a minor heart attack. He needs to eat better and exercise, but my mother is taking care of him," she told me.
"They're back together?" I asked.
"That I don't know. They seemed to be together when I left, but we'll see," she sighed.
"Were you able to talk to your mother about everything?"
"Yeah. She told me everything. We took a paternity test too. My dad is my dad," she smiled.
"That's great news. See, you were worried about nothing," I said and hugged her.
"My mother scared the fuck out of me. That shit had me stressed the fuck out," she whined.
"Oh I know. I've never seen you like that."
"Enough about me. When are we telling B he's gonna be a daddy?" she asked excitedly.
"I'm not. I need to know for sure."
"He's going to be so excited."
I threw my head back onto the pillow. She laughed.
"Please don't say anything to him Iris. Promise me," I pleaded.
"Your secret is safe with me. I will not tell my best friend that he is about to be a father until he tells me and then I will act surprised," she laughed.

"Ok pinky swear," I held out my pinky. She pinky swore and we laughed.
"Turn on the news," my roommate ran back into the room and turned on the TV.

It was a story about Sally's death. Apparently she left a video that was found on her computer. It gave details about everything she told Iris. They ended up taking 13 Senators, 6 lobbyists, and the district attorney of Maryland into the station for questioning.

"WOW!" Iris exclaimed.
"Did you know all of that?" I asked.
"Girl no and I'm so glad.
They probably would have tried to kill me too," she shrieked.
Her phone rang. It was Colin. She told him that we were watching the news and that she would be working from my apartment today. I know that he was calling just to check on her.
"He's so sweet!" I exclaimed.
"Whatever," she rolled her eyes.
"Seriously. I'm glad he got his act together. He's perfect for you," I replied.
"My parents are bugging me about grandkids. Colin wants a baby soon too," she sighed.
"Get pregnant so we can do this together," I said half joking.
She laughed at me and didn't respond. We continued to watch the news coverage.

They played bits and pieces of the video diary Sally left. She knew that she was going to die because she knew too much. She didn't tell Iris that she was dating one of the Senators at the heart of the scandal. That's how she had so much information and knew so many details.

"I bet he killed her," Iris stated.
"I bet he did too. Why would he want that to get out," I said.
A light bulb went off for the both of us.
"Are you thinking what I'm thinking?" Iris asked.
"Only if you're thinking that Seth killed Toni T.," I said.

"That's exactly what I'm thinking!" she exclaimed.

"It makes perfect sense. That guy told us that he saw a white man walk up and shoot her. If he had something going on with her, he would surely try to silence her ass," Iris continued.

"You think Toni was blackmailing him?" I asked.

"No, but I think when his wife was digging up his other infidelities she probably found out something about Toni too," she said.

"Then of course she told her mother who would have confronted Seth about it. Maybe they were all in on it," I said.

Iris sat up and looked at me. "Do you have the number to that detective that called me?" she asked.

"Bring my laptop over here. I will check my emails and voicemails," I told her. I remembered him leaving me a voicemail.

"Wait, what am I going to tell him?" she asked.

"Your theory."

"We have no proof though."

"That's why it's just a theory."

"You're right."

I found the number after a few searches and gave it to her. She dialed the number and hesitantly told the detective our theory.

"Put it on speaker," I whispered.

She pressed the speaker button and came closer to me.

She continued with the story and he listened intently. He never interrupted her.

"That's a hell of a theory but very plausible," he said after a few seconds of silence.

"I know it sounds crazy, but just check it out if you can," she pleaded.

"Will do Iris. I will keep you in the loop during the investigation. Just promise to call me if you get any proof," he told her.

"Will do," she hung up.

"What do you think?" I asked.

"Well hopefully they will do their due diligence. It is a high profile case so as long as it stays a relevant news story there will be pressure on them to solve it," she stated.

"This has been the craziest few months!" I exclaimed.

"Major understatement,' she seconded.

We ended up taking a nap for a few hours. So much for work! Iris phone rang and woke us up. It was B. He was asking if she knew where I was because he had been calling.

"She's right here. We fell asleep," she said shaking me awake. She told him that I wasn't feeling well due to some bad Thai food so she came over to keep me company. They talked for a few more minutes about her trip home and her father. She excitedly told him the news of the paternity test. I heard him say YES! through the phone. I smiled. I loved their friendship. They were more like brother and sister, not best friends. She hung up the phone and told me to call B when I was ready.
"I'm going to go home and curl up under my man," she said.
"Go make a baby," I laughed.
"Make sure you take those other tests. Text me the results," she snapped at me.
"Of course boss lady,' I laughed.
"Love you baby," she said waving on her way towards the door.
"Love you more baby," I yelled at her.

I picked up the bag and found two pregnancy tests inside. They were different brands. I decided to take them both. The wait was grueling. I decided to make a grilled cheese sandwich while I waited.
I don't know why I wanted one, but it was the best grilled cheese I had tasted. I went into the bathroom to check the tests. One was positive and one was negative. What the fuck? I wasn't going to worry about it.

I called my doctor's office and tried to make an appointment. They told me that the next available appointment was three weeks from now. I wanted to cuss them out, but I made the appointment and hung up the phone.

I felt a headache coming on. I laid down and went to sleep. I hoped that B would be happy when I finally told him. I decided not to tell him until I was absolutely certain. I didn't want to get his hopes up high, and I didn't know what I would do if his reaction was negative. I tried to sleep but those thoughts kept me up.

The rain hitting the window was beginning to annoy me. I usually like the sound of rain, but with this migraine every noise was irritating. It was also making me nauseous. Or was it something else? Today was such a crazy day. Two tests were positive, and then one came back negative. I don't even know if I'm pregnant, and my doctor can't see me for another three weeks. How can I go for three weeks without knowing if there is a baby in my womb? He doesn't even know, and I'm not sure I want to tell him. I've been pregnant before and lost the baby while I was in college and the symptoms I feel now are very similar. All I want to do is sleep, but I can't quiet these thoughts in my head.

I pulled the throw from the back of the couch and wrapped it around myself. The house was completely dark and I welcomed the silence. How did I even end up here? How could I have been so reckless?

The pounding in my head began to subside. Migraines are truly a pain from the deepest pits of hell. My phone beeped. Who in the hell could be texting me at 3 AM?

Bae: You up?
Me: Unfortunately
Bae: I want you.

That's all he ever had to say. That's why I'm in this predicament right now. I responded, "Come thru."

Then there was a knock on the door. I laughed out loud. He was truly something. I was already naked. Who sleeps in clothes? As soon as I opened the door, his eyes went to my breasts. "Hey," I said sheepishly, as if he had never seen me naked before.

"Hey," he replied, closing the door behind him. He pulled me close and held me in a tight embrace.
"I've missed you," he whispered in my ear. I felt so small in his arms. I rubbed my hands up and down his back and sighed. He made me feel so safe. We hugged for what seemed an eternity. I let him go and took his hand. I'm sure he wanted to head to the bedroom so I lead him there. There were no words. I undressed him slowly and kissed every inch of him while doing so. I was about to take off his underwear when he stopped me. "We don't have to have sex, I just want to hold you," he said taking me off guard.

He pulled me into the bed and held me closely. His arms engulfed my small frame. He was a giant compared to me. We laid in silence and I could feel his heartbeat on my back. I really wanted to tell him about the pregnancy, but I was afraid of what he would say. I wasn't sure how I even felt about it. I wrestled with these thoughts as I looked at the clock on the nightstand. It was 3:24 A.M.
He wasn't sleeping. His breathing didn't indicate sleep, so I decided to probe him. I turned around to face him. I rubbed his chest and had to talk myself into having this conversation.
"Hey you," I whispered. "Yeah," he replied. "Are you sleep?" I know, it's the dumbest fucking question to ask someone, but I was building up to drop this bomb. "No," he replied and began to rub on my back. My heart began to beat fast, and he pulled me closer, placing his hand on my chest. "I think I'm pregnant," I blurted out. "You are," he replied. Wait! What? I didn't even know what to say. I didn't say anything. He kissed me on my forehead and then said, "and it's a boy."

Chapter Thirteen: Proposal

I was so happy to get home to Colin. We had been through so much these past few weeks. Hopefully it was going to be all over soon. He hired Naschelle as his divorce lawyer and she immediately drew up papers that gave Carmen a lump sum and set up a trust fund for baby CJ. She put out an order for a paternity test and had Scott and her ex Kevin take the test. We were waiting for the results of that test. If Scott was CJ's father he was a no good friend. Colin told me that he would often confide in Scott about things and now he found out that all along he was fucking Carmen.

Colin was so calm about it too, too calm for my liking. I would have flipped out, but his thing was that they deserved each other and he didn't want to have anything else to do with them. I tipped my hat to him. I would have cooked up a revenge plot with the quickness. He just wanted the divorce to be over with and I really couldn't blame him.

I pulled into the garage and saw that the lights were off. Maybe he wasn't home yet. I parked and grabbed a bottle of wine to take into the house. I needed to restock my wine fridge from when my family was over. I opened the door and heard music playing. Yet, the house was completely dark. I put my bags down on the kitchen floor and placed the wine on the counter. Maybe Colin had fallen asleep to music.

When I turned the corner there was a trail of white and yellow rose petals with candles leading into the den.
"What is this?" I asked and followed the trail.
Colin was sitting in front of the fireplace with dinner and wine on a blanket.
"Aww this is sweet," I said and joined him on the blanket.

"I wanted to do something special for you," he embraced me. He smelled so good. He was wearing a tee shirt and basketball shorts. His usual around the house attire. I had on a jean dress.

"Let me help you out of that dress," he said.

He motioned for me to stand up and unbuttoned my dress. Luckily I had on a cute matching panty and bra set.

"Can I shower first?" I asked.

"No we have to celebrate," he handed me a glass of champagne.

"What exactly are we celebrating?" I asked.

"A miracle," he started.

"Hmmm," I said as I sipped the champagne.

"Well I'm not getting a divorce," he stated.

"Wait! What? How is that good news?" I asked shocked.

"Well I don't have to get a divorce because I was never legally married," he stated.

"What?" I asked. He was talking crazy.

"Well when Naschelle went to pull the marriage license and present it to the court there was no record of it," he said.

"Ok! Why is that?"

"If you stop interrupting me I could tell you." He shut me up quickly.

"The reverend never signed the marriage license or submitted it so we were never legally married," he continued.

I laughed. "Are you serious?"

"Crazy right?"

"Very crazy."

"Let's toast to that," he held his glass in the air.

We clinked glasses and drank all of the champagne. He filled our glasses up again.

"Since I was never married and don't have to wait for a divorce," he began nervously, "will you do me the honor of being the first and only Mrs. Mena?" he asked. He pulled out a beautiful yellow diamond ring.

"Yes, yes, yes!" I exclaimed and kissed him frantically. I straddled him and knocked him down onto the blanket. When I finally let him up for air he laughed.

"I was going to do a grand gesture with your friends and family, but I wanted it to be more intimate. More meaningful," he told me.
"It was perfect. The lead up was concerning, but it was a perfect proposal," I kissed him again.

"Great, now eat your lamb chops before they get cold," he commanded.
"You went to my favorite restaurant?" I asked surprised.
"It had to be a special dinner. Something we could tell our grandchildren about," he said feeding me a fork full of mashed potatoes.
"Mmmmm," I moaned.
"Oh, I'm gonna make you moan and scream all night Mrs. Mena," he kissed me on my neck.
"I can't wait Mr. Mena," I rubbed his head. We ate quickly and drank the rest of the champagne. Champagne always got me tipsy. Prince's Insatiable was playing on the speakers and I stood up and danced for him.
"That's what I like to see," he said and smacked me on my ass.
I danced until the song went off. I sat on his lap and kissed him from the top of his head down to his shorts.
"Take those off," I whispered. He undressed quickly.

"Let's go get in the Jacuzzi," I told him.
I took his hand and led him to the backyard.
We turned on the jets and waited for a few minutes, kissing the entire time. I hadn't had sex in my Jacuzzi yet and I wanted my first time to be with my future husband.
I took off my underwear and got in first.
"Bend over," he commanded.
I did as I was told and bent over with my arms folded on top of the Jacuzzi. He entered me from behind and lowered my body into the water. I was right over a jet so while he was inside of me there was a jet directly on my clit. I was in ecstasy.
"You like that huh?" he asked as he reached around and squeezed my nipples.

I came so quick and he did soon after. We laughed and just enjoyed the Jacuzzi and the warm summer night.

I was happy. My best friends were about to have a baby, my parents were working things out hopefully, and I was about to marry the most amazing man. I couldn't have asked for a happier ending.

Epilogue

A lot took place in a year. Seth and Robin Grier, Michael Lowenstein's daughter and son-in-law were convicted of murder. They hired a hit man to shoot Toni T because she was threatening to tell Michael Lowenstein about the affair she and Seth had a few years back. Since she wanted to start fresh with Michael, she figured she needed to come clean about everything. Unfortunately, her honesty got her killed. Seth and Robin both received 25 years. I was shocked because I just knew that her father would pull some strings to get her off, but he ended up making a public statement against her. Michael and his wife now had custody of their grandchildren.

The alderman's wife never confronted him about the footage we sent her. I guess she wanted to live in ignorant bliss. We still got paid, so it didn't matter.

There was never anyone convicted of Sally's murder, even though her death brought down one of the biggest sex trafficking rings in the United States.

Overall, I would say that business was good and my life took a turn for the better.

The south of France was amazing this time of year. We rented a yacht and had all of our friends and family join us on our honeymoon.
Our wedding ceremony was beautiful and intimate. We didn't want all of the hoopla of the a big formal wedding, we wanted only our closest friends and family there, plus B and Sasha had a huge wedding a few months back that was the talk of all the media for weeks.

Sasha looked gorgeous in her gown and B was beaming with pride. Their son, Bryant Jr., was pulled into the ceremony in a wagon. She was six months old when they got married. Now, he was 8 months and trying to walk.

I leaned over the railing and tried not to throw up. I was 3 months pregnant, but no one knew but Colin. It was not easy hiding my pregnancy since I was always sick. Luckily I wore my mother's wedding dress, which was loose around the stomach area.

"Mrs. Mena, I hope you found what you were looking for because I definitely did?" Colin whispered in my ear.

"Aww, those were the first words you ever spoke to me," I said turning around and wrapping my arms around his neck.
"I meant those words then, but now my dream has come true," he said kissing me.
"So has mine," I whispered.

"Hey, we're about to do a toast," B said interrupting us. We followed him into the eating area where everyone was gathered. My parents were there, my uncle, Naschelle and her new husband, B, Sasha, and Savannah and Colin's mother and sister were there as well.

They handed us glasses of champagne. I knew I would have to tell them I was pregnant because everyone would be expecting me to drink.
"Let's toast to the happy couple. To my best friend and sister Iris who has been to hell and back with me and brought my beautiful wife into my life. I wish you much success and love and to Colin, make sure you treat her right because I don't want to put the paws on you bruh," he laughed.
"To the beautiful bride and groom," my father interjected. Everyone echoed his sentiment.
"We have an announcement as well," Colin began. I looked at him knowing what he was about to say.

"In about four months we will be welcoming our baby boy into the world!" he exclaimed. There was applause, shrieks, and Hallelujahs from my mother. We were bombarded with hugs and words of love.

Indulgences could definitely turn into life-long commitments, and with the wrong partner they could be dangerous, but with the right one it could be the start of an amazing adventure.

THE END

Don't let the fun end here! Download the Spotify playlist that accompanies this novel. Scan the code below and enjoy!

Check out more titles by the Author
Available on Amazon

Spotify Playlist for Dangerous Indulgences

*<u>Read these books by friends of the Author
Available on Amazon</u>*